# Torn Pages

# Weird Bard Press

presents

# Torn Pages

Stories

of Social

Upheaval

Edited by Brandon H. Bell &
Christopher Fletcher

**Weirdbard Press**
Dallas | St. Louis
Please visit us on the web at
http://www.weirdbard.com

# Table of Contents

# Why Torn Pages?
by Brandon H. Bell

A more detailed version of this account may be found on the Weird Bard website, but for the sake of brevity I'm summarizing the genesis of the anthology you now hold.

On March 14th, 2013 I began a final exchange with ResponsiveEd/Quest, the publicly-funded charter school my daughter attended. Delany had come home with her copy of *The Diary of Anne Frank* damaged, page 130 torn out by the school. They'd done this to all copies of the book in their possession.

I emailed the superintendent and received this reply:

*Mr. Bell,*

*The book was for a school project in the classroom so I did not feel I needed to ask the parent regarding its use. I apologize. Had this been a personal copy you brought from, I certainly would have asked. I can refund you or purchase another book from half price books. Let me know your preference .*

*Thank you*

*Sent from my iPhone*

And my reply:

*Mrs. Y,*

*We'd like an undamaged copy returned to us. I would have been happy to sign a release form allowing my child to read the book (or not if I felt it inappropriate.) I would have even respected the decision not to teach a text that has difficult content.*

*Tearing pages out of books goes against everything we believe in. Source material is either appropriate or not. We should not change it to make it fit.*

*If you reconsider this policy of tearing pages out of books, we can do without a returned copy. That would be a real win that my daughter could feel good about.*

*The power of the word and all that. Otherwise Delany deserves an undamaged copy returned to her. If you think a used copy is the appropriate, that's your call.*

*Thanks,*

*Brandon Bell*

We received two replies, one from Mrs. Y, the school director, and one from Mrs. Z, Delany's teacher.

Mrs. Y:

*Thank you Mr. Bell for sharing your thoughts on this matter. I always appreciate hearing from parents. Certainly, I will discuss your concerns with my ELA teaching staff as we discuss novel options for next year. I apologize Delany was offended by the removal of a page from the book. Your suggestions will certainly be of consideration as we make a choice of novels for next year.*

*Thanks again for your input.*

*Mrs. Y*

Mrs. Z:

*Dear Mr. Bell,*

*I'm sorry we didn't let you know that we had planned on removing these pages from Delaney's Diary of Anne Frank book. Last year, these were pages that brought up concerns with parents, and so this year we removed them to do our best to protect the students and do what we thought was right for everyone. I thought that we had let parents know this at the beginning of the year, but my apologies if that was not communicated to you. We sure can replace the book if that is what you wish.*

*Sincerely,*

*Mrs. Z*

I thanked Mrs. Y and our interactions ended. She never

took action to replace the book or followed up in any other way. The teacher's reply felt honest and I thanked her:

> Mrs. Z,
>
> We appreciate your reply and sincerity.
>
> I mentioned to Mrs. Y that we'd prefer this policy be reversed (no more tearing pages out of books) but barring that, an undamaged copy will do.
>
> Some quick thoughts...
>
> This is the sort of practice that jumps out at me as simply wrong.
>
> And while I personally find it perplexing and sad that some parents are OK with their kids learning about the Holocaust, whereas the contents of page 130 are beyond the pale... I also understand you are left having to navigate that proverbial mine field.
>
> I hope someone there at Quest takes a stand. For instance:
>
> We're going to read this book, and we'll need permission slips to do so because it is mature at points. Those without permission will read Old Man and the Sea. (haha: that's what my 6th grade teacher did.)
>
> OR, We won't be reading XYZ at this grade level and defer it to a grade where the above is an option.
>
> Any book worth reading deserves the sanctity of each and every one of its pages.
>
> Thanks again for taking the time to reply.
>
> Sincerely,
>
> Brandon H. Bell

## Upstanders

The teacher, Mrs. Z, had this quote in her signature:

*"The more you read, the more things you will know.
The more that you learn, the more places you'll go."*
*-Dr. Seuss*

Let's just admit that anyone with this in their email signature is almost certainly one of the Good Guys™.

This would be the end of this story. We'd decided to take Delany out of Quest once testing was done. She'd enter the new school where we'd recently moved for one month before summer. We hoped she'd make some friends before the end of the semester. This is life, right? You try to stand up for what matters even when others, right up to the folks who are in places of authority, act as though your concerns are baseless and frivolous. And in the end, you effect no change, the machine churns on. Maybe your kids see that you took that stand and that counts for something.

But the story didn't end there.

At the end of their reading of *Anne Frank*, the school had a field trip scheduled to visit the Holocaust Museum. We felt some conflict over her going on the field trip–How will they edit this experience?–Big sister Chelsea went as a chaperon so Delany had some support from home.

The tour culminated in a talk given by a Holocaust survivor. His family, like Anne Frank's, was hidden by another family. I wish I could give more details of his story, but I only know it second hand. One comment stuck out to Chelsea and she thought it might have hit Mrs. Z as well, given her subsequent actions.

Teary-eyed, impassioned, this gentleman admonished his listeners to pay attention. To see when something unjust takes place. To say something. Even if it seems small. Even if it seems no good will come of it. Don't be a bystander, he said, be an upstander.

While they proceeded from the museum, Mrs Z. stopped our girls and handed Delany a copy of *The Diary of Anne Frank* she'd just purchased from the museum book store. Your family, she told her, was the only one that said anything about the torn pages.

You can google what is on page 130 of *The Diary of Anne Frank*, the practice of tearing that page from the book is so prevalent. It doesn't matter what is on the page, it is a small part of her experience. It is the truth. And any attempt to alter it is wrong. We prepared this anthology that takes this circumstance and others like it as a prompt.

It is time. Ideologues who believe they know best how history and literature and science should be presented to students are hard at work. We believe the light of understanding and discernment needs to shine upon these folks. We believe pages should never be torn from books. We believe no filter, religious or otherwise, should be placed on the secular classroom.

And we believe this stance is uniquely positioned to protect and respect the concerns of pluralistic society. We'll all be the better for it.

We believe there is more understanding for us to find and we present these stories as a small contribution to the unending search.

# Do You Have a Weapon, Sir?
by H.S. Donnelly

B oarding pass," the flight attendant said, eyes fixed on the surface of her console. Her fingers flitted across, tapping here, then there.

The Flight Gal's dark blue uniform was neatly pressed. Likewise, her hair, makeup and lipstick were firmly in place. I wondered how she had fallen into this career. Had she been infatuated with travelling? If so, that gloss had rubbed off long ago, one passenger, one flight, one airport stopover at a time.

I placed my boarding pass in front of her:

> *Passenger: Wong, Paul*
> *Economy Class. Breakfast Snack.*
> *Charlotte NC to Chicago IL, 2 Hours.*
> *Layover, 1 Hour.*
> *Chicago IL to St. Louis MO, 1 Hour 45 Minutes.*

She picked it up and flicked it against her reader until it beeped and electronically slotted me into the plane. Looking up she said, "We can give you a middle seat, sir."

Ugh. "Is there an aisle or window available?"

"No sir."

Pause. "Sure."

"Thank you, sir." More tapping, then she went through the usual list of questions until she reached the last one, "And do you have a weapon, sir?"

"No."

"Do you wish to rent one, sir?"

"No."

She looked startled, then made a small gesture to her left and said quietly, "Would you mind standing over there, sir?"

I nodded.

10

It was all part of flying nowadays. That, and flying northwest to Chicago where I would re-plane onto a flight that would finally take me south to where I was going.

A heavy man stood next in line, fifty-ish, clean-shaven, intense blue eyes. Tight. Enclosed. A type of guy, I figured, used to giving orders. Never asking for things, just reaching. And smiling faintly at jokes to fit into the conversation. His only genuine laughter would occur at his Saturday night poker games where he would drink shots of whisky and give a harsh hah-hah laugh at all the off-color jokes.

He glanced at me. Curious as to why I had been told to stand aside? Or another frazzled passenger trying to get to where he was going?

*Get to where you are going.*

Yeah, that just about sums it up. In the 50's everyone described it as *arriving at your destination.* Sounded sophisticated: Cary Grant, Grace Kelly, champagne glasses and all that. Today we're just relieved to *get to where we're going.*

Once more Flight Gal concluded her routine with, "And do you have a weapon, sir?"

The man slipped back his suit jacket, revealing a small pistol in a light-brown leather holster. It was probably a *1911 R1 Carry.* Like the commercial said, *"The right heft for the on-the-go businessman . . ."*

"Thank you, sir," Flight Gal responded, and her attention swivelled back to her work surface.

He bent down, grabbed the handle of his carry-on luggage, tossed me a parting *Huh* look and then strode towards the gateway door, his small bag wheeling after him like a little dog.

Two passengers later, she turned her attention back to me and, in well-practiced airport-ese, asked, "Sir, is there a reason why you do not wish to carry a weapon onto this flight?"

"I don't believe in carrying a gun." Over the years, I had found this was all I had to say.

"Very well sir," her expression remained frozen, "you need to sign this waiver. It advises that you assume all risks if you choose to board this flight unarmed. Thumb print?" She pointed to a digit-reader attached to her work-surface.

"No, I'll just sign it." Like a lot of things they make you do at the airport, this was a bit of a charade. So I was happy to waste her time for a change.

"Very well, sir." She pressed her lips into a tight line, her expression changing to, *Come on fella, we have an airport to run here.* She touched her work-surface and a form slid out from the side of her console.

I scrawled my signature on it, not that it mattered. According to flight statistics, ninety four point seven percent of my fellow passengers would be armed today. So me being unarmed didn't make a whole lot of difference.

"Thank you, sir. Have a safe flight."

Sure.

I picked up my bag and headed towards the gate door, passing the flight insurance dispensing machine. The Rock of Gibraltar Insurance Company must have paid a pretty penny for that location; the last chance to prey upon nervous passengers. Of course, anyone reading the fine print would have realized that *Armed Insurrection* was not one of the *All Perils* covered.

Arriving at the back of the boarding line, I stopped,

waiting, waiting, for those already on the plane to shove their hand luggage into overhead compartments and side-step into their seats. But I wasn't concerned. Since we were The Checked In, no matter how long it took, we would not be left behind. The line moved forward in stops and starts until, at last, I crossed over the threshold and onto the plane.

Self-absorbed business men and women populated the cabin along with a few holidaying families and a full complement of flight attendants, including two muscular looking Air Marshalls, one tall, black, the other shorter, Korean, standing together with their arms folded, quietly conversing while scanning the passenger cabin. The only thing missing were the dark sunglasses.

At last, I reached my seat, the aforementioned middle one. I glared at it. The gun toting guy from check-in filled the aisle seat.

Pistol Pete gave me an *Oh, you again* look.

I opened the overhead and—Oh my lucky day!—my bag fit when I shoved it in. Then, as part and parcel of this whole ritual, Pistol Pete stood up and let me shuffle to my seat.

Just as I sat down, a thin, elderly woman stopped in the aisle. "Excuse me," she said, pointing a finger towards the window. "I think that's my seat."

Her grey hair was permed. She wore a sleek yellow dress accented by a blue necklace. Someone's grand-mother off to visit family? Or maybe to see a specialist in another city about a medical condition, though, on second thought, she seemed too relaxed for that.

"No problem ma'am," Pistol Pete said as he stood up. Then it was my turn to shuffle out.

"Sorry," she offered.

13

"It's the way they design these planes," I said.

"Of course. By the way, my name's Ruth."

"Paul," I said.

Pistol Pete turned, "And I'm Glen, since we're doing introductions."

We settled ourselves in, and, naturally, my phone rang.

My wife, Gail.

"Yes dear," I said, "I'm fine . . . Yes, everyone is armed . . . No one looks crazy . . . Yes, someone near me has a weapon . . ." I glanced at Pistol Pete. "No, he doesn't look like he's about to use it—Hey, the plane is about to take off. Got to hang up now. Airline safety rules . . . Yes, I love you too . . . Yes, I'll call you when I get to Chicago."

The last hijacking of a U.S. flight occurred twelve years earlier, with all four of the perpetrators, three crew and sixteen passengers being killed in a wild melee of gunfire. Still, it had been hailed as proof positive that a determined group of airline passengers could foil a terrorist attack.

Pistol Pete shifted. His gun nudged against me. "Sorry," he muttered. "I can put it on my left if you like. I can pull it out from either side."

"That's okay," I replied. "Besides, I don't think you'll be using it."

"Well hard to say. Those On-Line Passenger Personality Questionnaires are so easy to fake. And," he tapped his jacket over where his gun was, "I wanna be ready."

"I guess," I said.

He turned towards the front of the plane and we lapsed into an agreed-upon silence.

A flight attendant walked up, stopped and stood there head cocked, waiting. Then the safety video began and she went through her motions.

*Please turn off all electrical devices . . .*

*Keep your firearm holstered unless you feel your life is in imminent peril . . .*

*In the event of an emergency, your oxygen mask will drop down . . .*

*To inflate your life vest . . .*

*Remember, our cabin crew is here to take care of all your safety concerns.*

Then the Captain came on, "Ladies and gentlemen, we're just about ready for takeoff . . . Weather's clear all the way to Chicago . . . So please settle back and relax . . . And let's keep it in the holster today, Okay?"

There was a slight titter throughout the cabin.

Then the roar of the engines began. The runway, trees and buildings slid by slowly, then faster and faster. The acceleration pushed me back into my seat. The rumble of the wheels stopped as the plane attained takeoff speed. The cabin tilted upwards and climbed. Come on, clear the fence at the end of the runway . . . Now the highway . . . Okay, now get over those low rent apartment buildings just beyond the height restriction zone . . .

The plane banked. Through the window, I could just see the streets and highways tilting away. Finally the plane reached cruising altitude  and the seat belt sign turned off.

I relaxed my grip on my chair's arm rests.

The Captain came on again to tell us to remain buckled up anyway.

"Excuse me," Ruth touched my arm.

I answered, "Yes?"

She looked at me with wide-open eyes. "Are you not carrying a-a gun with you?"

"No."

15

"Do you not like guns, then?"

"No," I replied and, not wishing to sound rude, added, "There was a gun fatality in my family some years ago." Not exactly true. But I'd found that this answer stopped any further inquiries.

"Oh sorry," her hand went up to her mouth, "I didn't mean to pry."

"It's all right," I pretended, "it happened a long time ago."

"Well, I'm still sorry for you," she said, then paused, seemingly about to say something else.

I waited.

"Oh . . . I know we're not supposed to pull these out," she said, "but my son insisted I get this." She reached into her handbag and lifted out a snub-nosed pistol with a bright pink handle; the small, stylish ones targeted at the female demographic. "I wasn't very comfortable with it. But Henry insisted."

"May I ask if you got some training?" Pistol Pete asked, leaning over and intruding into my space.

"Oh yes. My son took me out to the shooting range a couple of times. But I felt a bit foolish. After all," she smiled, "I can't imagine ever shooting anyone. Still, it makes him feel I'm safe."

"Your son's smart. Training's important. A fool with a gun is worse off than a fool with no gun. I got some good training in the military—Say, is that the new LC9 model?"

"I couldn't tell you. Here, have a look—" As she passed it, she lost her grip and the gun fell with a distinct thud between my feet.

"Oh dear!" she said.

"It's okay, it's okay," I said as I quickly bent down and searched the floor. I found it and picked it up. "Here—"

16

Thump. Thump. Thump.

"Freeze!"

I looked up. The Korean Security Dude was pointing a Glock 45 at me. And he looked pretty snarly, too.

"Put the gun down—slowly," Security Dude ordered.

I felt my stomach giving way as I stared into the gun barrel. I swallowed, carefully placed the gun on my arm rest and raised my hands.

A dozen people had drawn their weapons using the top of their own seat, or the seat in front of them, to brace their arms.

Thump. Thump. Thump.

His co-worker arrived from the rear of the plane, likewise with drawn weapon. "Everyone reholster! Reholster!" he shouted. "The situation is secure."

There were scattered sighs of relief as those who had ducked peered up, and the shooters glanced around to see who else had drawn.

"No, no," Pistol Pete interjected, "this guy didn't—"

"Sir!" Black Security Dude said, "I am dealing with a situation! So I have to ask you to very slowly get out of your seat, now!"

Pistol Pete stopped talking, got up from his seat and edged backwards into the aisle.

"Now you, sir," Security Dude motioned slightly with his gun for me to move into the aisle.

"Please, he wasn't—" Ruth began.

"Don't worry, ma'am. He won't hurt you. The situation is contained."

Ruth deflated into a ball of resignation.

"Stand up on your tippy-toes and put both your hands behind your back!"

I did as ordered. He pulled out some plastic handcuff

17

bands and tightened them around my wrists.

His partner picked up the gun, holding it as if it was the remains of a dead rabbit.

"A pink handle!" a young fellow sitting three rows back chortled. He was dressed in surplus army fatigues; either trying to look cool, or just not having enough money to buy more normal clothing. "Girlie-Boy!" the guy next to him guffawed.

Oh God, I thought, so now I am being outed.

But the joke fell flat as the rest of the cabin was too busy being on heightened alert.

"Eddie, take him up front. There'll be more room," Black Security Dude said.

"Right. This way," Eddie held my head downwards and marched me into First Class.

All eyes in the cabin followed me as I was paraded forward.

Hell of a way to be upgraded, I thought.

"Ladies and gentlemen," the Captain came on, "I've had to declare a Security Incident in accordance with F.A.A. Regulation blah-blah-blah. Consequently we are being diverted to the Blue Grass Airport in Lexington until we're cleared to continue."

There was a scattering of groans.

The First Classers turned as we parted the drapes and a few people began reaching down.

But Eddie cut them off at the pass. "Everything is under control, here," he said calmly. "Please keep your weapons holstered."

People went back to what they were doing, though some kept glancing at us.

"Sit down," Eddie ordered, steadying me as I sat.

Whoa, I thought to myself, as I plopped into a rather

plush, roomy seat.

Eddie stood over me. "What's your name?" he demanded.

He seemed like the sort who might—Oh Hell, I didn't know anything about this guy. For all I knew he might go home and arrange flowers, or fire up his game console and spend all night playing Grand Theft Auto Teenage Zombie Warrior.

"Paul Wong." I answered.

He had already clicked open his comm. "Hi Olaf," he said, "I got the guy here . . . Yeah, I'll check." He turned to me. "You got some ID?"

"Driver's license?"

"Yeah."

"Back pocket. In my wallet."

I shifted a bit and he pulled out my wallet and opened it. "Here it is, Olaf. North Carolina issue." He read out the number. ". . . Yeah, he's got a credit card. Might as well do that too." He gave that too. "Yeah, I'll ask." He lowered the comm. "And we'd like to get your finger prints, too."

"Do I have to give you that?"

"No, but things will go quicker if you do. 'Cause otherwise I'll have to call a judge and get a warrant. F.A.A. Regulation blah-blah-blah gives us the authority to . . ." And he gave me way, way too much information as to the legal rigmarole backing up everything he could possibly do to me.

"Whatever," I said.

I turned over somewhat and let him take my finger prints.

"Thanks. And I guess we'll take some DNA, while we're at it. Hair sample will do." He pulled out a tiny pair of nail clippers and snipped a bit of hair from the side of my head.

"What do you do with my DNA?"

"We log it into a database."

"Do you ever look at it?"

"Only if we're looking for a DNA match."

Eddie picked up the comm again. "Olaf, any progress? . . . Okay, I'll ask." He turned to me, looking more intently. "Mr. Wong, have you ever lived in Tucson?"

"No."

"He says 'no' . . . Have you ever met a man named Sanfred Diego Charles?"

"I've never heard of him."

"Have you ever been involved with or voted for 'The American Night Watch Party'?"

"No."

"Can we check your voting record?"

"What?"

"How you voted in elections. We track the information, but we need your permission to look at it."

"What's next? Check to see if I ever snuck into the 'Eight or Less' grocery line with nine items?"

"Please, Mr. Wong," Eddie's expression morphed into 'Concerned'. "I'm just doing my job here. Really, we don't care whether you voted Republican or Democratic. All we want to see is if you ever supported certain fringe parties."

"I never vote for third parties as it is a waste of time."

"Do we have your permission?"

"Yeah, go ahead."

"Thank you, Mr. Wong. Olaf, go ahead . . . Okay, we'll talk when we land . . . Yeah, have a good day, too."

He clicked off his comm and turned to me. "Okay, you don't have much of a record. So I'll take the cuffs off." He pulled out a knife. "Just roll over onto your side again."

I did and he cut the plastic off.

"So," he continued, "let's go over what happened. You began by pulling out your gun—"

"No."

He gave me a questioning look.

"The old lady next to me pulled out her gun to show it to Pist—the guy on the other side."

"Why did she do that?"

"He asked if it was a new model of gun and she was passing it over to let him have a look."

"But that is in contravention to F.A.A. regulations."

"Yes."

"So why did you end up with the gun?"

"She dropped it—"

His eyes bugged out.

"And I was picking it up because it fell between my feet."

"Dylan," he called.

The Black Security Dude had shown up and poked his head through the curtain.

"This guy says it was the old lady's gun."

"Yeah," Dylan glanced at me, "it sure looked like a lady's gun." His eyebrows arched slightly as he said this.

"Bring the old lady up here. And then the guy in the aisle seat. I want to find out why he wanted her gun."

"No, he has his own gun—" I started to say. But this Dylan character had already disappeared.

I passed a rather frightened Ruth being led forward as I headed back to my seat. I gave her a brief smile, though she didn't notice.

Pistol Pete looked at me as I got to our row.

"You're next," I said, not caring if I sounded mischievous.

He gave me a surly look.

Ruth came back ten minutes later and so it was Pistol Pete's turn.

"This is all my fault," Ruth said softly. "I've gotten everyone in trouble and the darn airplane is going to land in Lexington, of all places!"

"Spilt milk," I replied.

"But I told them you didn't have anything to do with it!"

"Thanks."

Pistol Pete was back in record time. Perhaps being ex-military had something to do with it.

"I'm so dreadfully sorry," Ruth repeated.

Pistol Pete sighed. "These things happen. Don't worry. We'll land. They'll question us. And that will be the end of it."

Ruth peered out the window. "You know, there's a jet flying awfully close to us."

Both of us looked. Indeed, there was a fighter jet.

"F-35 escorting us," Pistol Pete said. "Standard procedure."

"Because ..." Ruth started to say, then stopped.

"'Fraid so."

"Oh crap ..."

It looked like she needed a good hug. But airline passenger seats, seat belts and all; well, you know.

I grasped her hand instead.

So we sat there. Flight Gal walked by, looking left and right, carefully eyeing each row of passengers. She gave me an extra hard stare. They hadn't rolled out the beverage cart due to the security alert and I'm sure I wasn't alone missing that rather unpalatable cup of airline coffee.

The plane tilted downwards, the seat belt signs came on and, for good measure, the pilot again came on to tell us to do them up. We taxied and stopped some distance from the terminal . . . and sat and waited.

The airplane door opened and I could hear muffled talking. Then Flight Gal reappeared, leading two guys and a gal, all outfitted in Homeland Security uniforms. The woman and one of the men were sporting AA-12 assault shotguns. They stopped at our row.

"Them," Flight Gal said, pointing.

"Thanks," the unarmed man said. "You three. Up." And we marched off the plane in glorious fashion.

It was not much of a terminal and the room they put me in was pretty nondescript. Cheap looking table. Four utilitarian chairs. Small window looking out onto the grass and then the runway. A bunch of black-and-white pictures of old propeller-driven planes on the far wall.

I waited, thoroughly tired and pissed off. Funny how not carrying a gun usually kept me out of trouble.

The door opened and two authority figures came in. The older one, stoop-shoulders, glasses, balding, smiled. The other one, military uniform, solidly built, looked impassively at me. Neither appeared armed, but I was sure both were carrying concealed.

"Hello," baldy said, "I'm Major Salatino. I'm with the Security Service." He extended his hand.

"Hello," I shook it, surprised.

"Would you like a coffee? I understand they didn't serve any on the plane."

"Sure."

"Sergeant?" Salatino motioned towards the door with his head.

"Yes sir."

He sat down and opened an old fashioned notebook and laid it on the table. "Well . . ." he let out his breath.

"I guess you've had quite a day."

"Yes."

"And you were travelling to . . ."

"St. Louis via Chicago. A presentation for my company that I will be missing."

Salatino nodded. "I see. Do you want to call anyone?"

"I did that just after we got off the plane."

"Good, good."

The coffee arrived and after more small talk, Salatino got down to business. "Mr. Wong, we wanted to talk to you to understand what happened so we can review our procedures and see if there is anything we can improve upon."

"Right." I wondered how much of this was B.S.

"So maybe you can tell us from your own perspective what exactly happened."

"Well . . ." I began, and once more started into my story—

"Whoa!" Salatino held up a hand. "You weren't carrying a gun?"

"Yes."

He tapped into his notebook and then looked back up at me with a stern expression. "Is there a reason why you weren't armed?"

I knew my routine answer wouldn't wash here. "I didn't grow up in a 'gun culture'. I've never owned a gun and," I paused, staring down at my outstretched palms, "I feel perfectly safe almost all the time without one."

Now it was his turn to sigh. "I'm afraid I can't let you re-plane."

"What!" I was on my feet before I realized it. "Are you telling me I can't fly unless I carry a gun? Do you know how stupid that—"

24

"Please, Mr. Wong!" Salatino raised his voice, "Sit down."

Reluctantly, I obeyed.

"This isn't about 'guns' or 'no guns'. This is about restricting people who have abnormal personality profiles. Academic studies have proved that mentally unbalanced people cause most security incidents on planes—"

"Are you accusing me of being a crazy?"

At this, his body edged back. "No, no, Mr. Wong. But you have to admit it sounds peculiar that someone who claims to avoid guns nonetheless was caught with one—"

"It was the old lady's gun," I said, too loud. Then calming down, I continued, "She was passing it to the guy on the other side of me and dropped it!"

"Oh?"

I stood up again. "This is outrageous! I'm calling my Congressman over this! My Senator! The President! The—The—" and I ran out of people to call.

"Please, Mr. Wong—"

"My lawyer!" I threw in, although at this instant I didn't have one.

"Mr. Wong! I'll see what I can do here!" Salatino stood up, grabbed his notebook and quickly left the room.

I sighed and sat down once more. The other guy had his eyes trained on me. Maybe he thought I would jump him. I didn't know. Okay, I thought, staring contest! I settled into my seat and stared back.

Ten minutes later, Salatino was back. "Okay, you can get on the plane. But you should think carefully about the consequences of flying unarmed."

"Thanks."

Fifteen minutes later I was back on the plane. Pistol Pete was already in his seat with his tablet out. He was reading some sort of report.

"Excuse me," I said.

He looked up. "Oh, sorry." He stood up and let me in.

I resumed my seat. The window seat was empty.

The pilot came on, "Ladies and gentlemen, thank you very much for enduring this unscheduled delay. We will be departing immediately. Cabin crew, prepare for takeoff."

The plane began rolling forward.

"Where's Ruth?" I asked.

"Gone," Pistol Pete said, head down.

I glanced over at the now vacant window seat. "Do you think she'll end up on the No Fly List?"

"Maybe, though they might just give her a good talking to and remove her right to carry a firearm onto an airplane. Her son will probably be having kittens by now. Sad. You really should have just left the weapon on the floor."

"Me? What about you asking about her gun?"

Pistol Pete glanced up from his tablet, pressing his lips together. "Yeah, I should have told her to put it away. My bad, I guess." His shoulder went up slightly, suggesting the conversation was over.

After a couple of minutes I added, "Well, I sort of ratted on her during my interview."

"How she was passing the gun?"

"Yeah. I feel bad about that, 'cause she didn't mean any harm."

Pause. Then, "Understood. You had to tell your story. Anyway . . ." and he turned back to his tablet.

Once into the air, Dylan and Eddie were even more visible, continuing to stroll up and down, checking out everyone in each row. And the flight attendants displayed their holstered PP-L pistols more prominently as they went about their business offering drinks and snacks.

The price of eternal vigilance, I thought, is more eternal vigilance.

I opened up my tablet and started integrating data from a spreadsheet into my presentation. But it was pointless since the presentation was already over. I gave up and let my head slump back onto the headrest.

"Would you like coffee, soft drinks, peanuts?" a flight attendant's voice asked.

I stirred.

"Hey, uh, Paul, you want anything?" Pistol Pete asked.

I blinked and straightened up in my seat. "Yeah, coffee would be fine Pist—er, Glen."

"Cream and sugar?" the steward asked. He smiled that reflexive grin that must be stamped onto their faces during training. But he seemed to be a pleasant, low key sort of guy. This was probably the start of a long fourteen hour shift made even longer by this security incident. So it would be very late by the time he finished flying all the way across the country. And of course he would see none of it, save for airport gates. We all are run off our feet these days.

"Just milk, please."

"Here," Glen handed it to me.

"Thanks."

The pilot came on again as we descended, "Ladies and gentlemen, we will be landing shortly in Chicago. The cabin crew hopes you have had a pleasant flight and we look forward to having you fly with us again soon. For those of you continuing on to Toronto from Chicago, that flight is carried out under International Flight Rules. So those carrying a weapon must surrender it."

There were scattered groans around the cabin, as at least a few people didn't like the idea of flying unarmed.

"Fortunately," the pilot continued, "the airline provides a Weapons Safe Storage Program where, for a modest fee, you can check your weapon with us in Chicago and then pick it up on your return flight."

"Another cash grab," Glen muttered.

Right on.

The plane finally stopped and the seat belt sign went off. We stood up and retrieved our luggage. Glen got his carry-on, then nodded to me. "Well, it's been nice flying with you."

I stopped. Recovering from my surprise, I said, "Yeah, same here."

"By the way, I have an old Smith & Wesson stowed in my carry-on that I don't really like anymore. If you want some protection with you on your next leg, I'd be happy to give it to you."

"No," I shook my head, "thanks."

He paused, then said, "Understood. Well, good luck getting to where you're going."

"You too."

# Mitty Starving Dog
# Ghost Dances the White Away

by Marissa James

M itty Starving Dog had never been a good dancer. Neither kind, powwow or club dancing. I think he stopped dancing at powwows when he was eight, and like the rest of us didn't get out enough to do much of the other kind. Which was funny because he liked to, you know? He told me so enough times. But you don't need to be good at something to enjoy it, and you don't always like the things you're good at.

Mitty in a nutshell. He couldn't follow the rhythm of the drums or the logic of the steps. And yet somehow he taught us all to Ghost Dance.

Last time the Ghost Dance happened before Mitty was around 1900. A prophet called Wovoka had a vision that spread to tribes all through the west. They danced the Ghost Dance thinking it would save them from colonization. It would call up the ancestors and they'd boot the whites out, or the earth would open wide and swallow our problems. Or something.

They tried it at Wounded Knee. Obviously, it didn't work. Growing up on the Res—the West Idaho Indian Reservation—made this pretty clear.

But Mitty. The first time he Ghost Danced was on the side of a dusty freeway for a cop. He was driving fine but so what? You put one little, two little, three little teenage Indians in a car, it's what happens.

I sat in the back seat, and his little sister Becka in the front. Mitty acted pleasant as pie to the cop, who had a face like chewed-up asphalt and, when he leaned through the window to look at me, breath to match.

When the cop told him to get out me and Becka knew we were in trouble. Not because Mitty couldn't walk a straight line, but because the cop had crooked eyes.

I stared at Mitty's sneaker-clad feet through the rear

window, thinking very straight-lined thoughts, when they started to move. Not in a straight line, or any line at all, but a weave. A pattern. An ancient way that I was seeing for the first time.

"We're screwed," I said. Becka moaned in her throat. Of all times to remember the way you'd powwow danced when you were eight—

I glanced at the cop, expecting to see him with handcuffs ready. Or maybe his sidearm, because sure as shit this could be classified as a threatening gesture, if you were the sort of cop who maintained a special, color-sensitive definition of what was threatening.

Instead a dumb look marred his face, then, poof. A cop-shaped outline flickered on my vision. He was gone and I jumped so bad my head hit the roof.

Mitty stilled. Me and Becka debated whether it was okay, then we got out, looked around. Nothing but us, and Mitty looking as confused as we were, and an empty cop car, lights still wheeling up top.

"What did you do?" Becka demanded.

"Shit if I know," Mitty said, pushing back his long hair. His round face slack, and his eyes like quarters. "But I guess I ain't getting a ticket."

"Let's get out of here," I said.

He frowned, then nodded and got back behind the wheel and drove.

.

Took a couple days but I convinced him to teach me. Meaning that when a pair of state cops came looking for Mitty Starving Dog to ask him about a certain traffic stop, we Ghost Danced them into thin air together.

Word got around after that. I taught some of the other

33

guys and girls from school. Soon everyone, kids and older folks, wanted in too. Didn't have to ask me twice. Some were worried they'd poof out of existence when I showed them how to Ghost Dance but that wasn't the way it worked. The Ghost Dance was ours, it had been meant to protect us, so naturally we were immune.

We got the dance down to a science, on the Res in the middle of gray hills and blowing grit, rusting pickups and punched up basketballs. Talked about it, thought about it, but for a long time didn't do much else. Because even though no one said it, everyone knew what the next step would be.

Mitty's uncle Charles said what everyone was hungry to hear. Charles, who'd blown off most of his pointer finger in a hunting accident so that when he tried to flash a peace sign people took it for something else, unless they knew him.

He wagged that stump of a finger at a bunch of us and said, "Ghost Dancing ain't meant for sitting around doing nothing. It's how we're supposed to get back our land, ain't it?"

"But this is Mitty's Ghost Dance, not Wovoka's," I said, tasting a lack of conviction in the words. Really I wanted to know what we could do with it. I had a couple ideas brewing already.

"Yeah," Mitty said. "I can't even show my face in Astor anymore, can I? Or more cops are going to go missing and it'll just get worse."

Charles shook his head. "I don't know how you think it works, boy. They'll send more cops out here after you, and what? You're going to Ghost Dance them all one at a time? It ain't going to stop unless you stop it."

Mitty stared at his cracked sneakers and didn't speak

34

though the rest of us, standing on the saggy porch or leaning against the rails or sitting on the stoop, waited on his word. Waited for him to say that we deserved some respect for once. The world needed to stop pushing us to the margins of the past—and the present. We shouldn't be footnotes, afterthoughts, have-nots. Not anymore. And the Ghost Dance was our way of making this possible. Wasn't this why it had come to Mitty?

We waited. I waited. Mitty shifted his gaze to the hills.

"How many people is Astor again?" I asked, thinking of the nearest town. If Mitty couldn't step up someone had to.

"Not more than five hundred people," Jerome said.

"All right," I said. Gave Mitty one more chance to step in, but he was silent, watching the hills as though they were supposed to answer for him. "Then let's do it."

Everyone on the Res could Ghost Dance by then, including my mom and little sister and Judd Candlefish, who was old enough he'd known people who told stories about Wovoka's Ghost Dance. He danced as well as anyone, as though he'd been doing it forever.

For us Ghost Dancing was as natural as breathing.

If Mitty was our divinely inspired prophet, well, I'd been right beside him from the beginning, so I became the unofficial dance leader. War chief? I couldn't help thinking it amounted to the same thing. And I wouldlead us on Astor. At least ours would be a peaceful war, a nonviolent purge.

A bloodless coup.

We planned, but a town that size didn't require too much in the way of planning. We started at the outskirts, synchronized our watches, and danced our way into town in the span of a half hour. Beating hand-drums and tying bells to our ankles to keep time. The town of Astor fell. Or, its population did. Anyone who wasn't one of us got Ghost Danced away, wiped up like a stain, removed like a sloughed-off scab. Easy as that. All of us dancers met in the middle of town, panting and sweating under the only traffic light, and surveyed the empty cars and shops and sidewalks.

Something more powerful than electricity buzzed in the silent air. Something more ancient than the Ghost Dance.

We'd made our point.

Or had we? Astor was a nowhere town, tiny and point-less, who'd know it was gone? It would just be a ghost town a little newer than the others dotting the dead hills around the Res.

The houses and cars and TV reception in Astor were better than ours had been back at home, so the town became our base of operations. Mitty would've gone back if we didn't all convince him how much we needed him. Who were we, and how could we plan our next step, without our prophet close?

We started thinking about Coeur D'Alene, or Boise, or Spokane. Something people would notice if it was gone. We settled on Creighton, the nearest place with shopping malls and car lots and plentiful fast food joints. We called distant relatives, and they called more distant ones, and folks started showing up from a good ways to learn the Ghost Dance. I didn't have time to teach now so I left it to the other guys; I was too busy Googling street maps and printing them out one section at a time and pinning them up on the walls of my ratty new house, which smelled like old lady and dog breath. When I ran out of ink I raided other houses for their printers and paper, too, until I had

36

a stack of the machines. Like war trophies I kept them all.

Mitty didn't do much except worry we were going to get killed; if not shot by cops, or run down by farm workers in dinged up trucks, then the army or air force was going to notice us pretty soon and drop bombs on our asses. It seemed like a valid point, until his uncle Charles reminded us that Wovoka's Ghost Dancers had worn shirts meant to make them impervious to gunfire.

We didn't have any such shirts. We did have cracked sneakers, dirt-dyed athletic shoes, peeling plastic sandals, fading faux leather combat boots. Whatever. If we'd danced in them the first time we kept wearing them like lucky underwear, never taking them off or changing them out. Hoping the good dance vibes would protect us.

Mitty complained that his sneakers felttoo tight, too frayed, though they looked to be holding up as well as anybody's.

Seeing as no bombs dropped or missiles launched, it must've been working. Then again, in this country's experience, Indians stopped being a problem if you ignored them. Maybe that's what was up.

Ignoring us wouldn't be possible much longer.

With our volunteer militia piling in, the population of Astor grew to double, then triple, what it had been before we danced it under. It got crowded. Me and some of the other guys organized troops or squadrons or teams of dancers and worked out their courses, though we couldn't agree what we were calling them. There were only so many ways into the city, only so many neighborhoods, and we'd established the effect radius of the Ghost Dance with Astor to be a couple of blocks around the person doing the dancing, and exponentially more with additional dancers. We'd also watched plenty of war movies in the meantime to pound out our strategy.

It wasn't too long and we were ready.

A couple thousand Indians dancing on a city from all sides couldn't have really scared anyone. At first. We danced in the backs of pickup trucks, secured in the beds by rope or bungee cords, in the hours before dawn as we were driven into the city center in fleets. It seemed as effective as anything.

I led the dance from the west, Becka driving, and Mitty with his uncle Charles came in driving from the south. We'd meet up somewhere in downtown.

Not a half hour into it my dancers came upon a roadblock; cop cars clogging the freeway from one side to the other, lights whirling in their own dance, megaphone voices threatening us to stop or else.

We urged our pickup chargers forward with war cries of our own devising. A couple of the guys started doing the Cleveland Indians tomahawk chop and the call that went with it and from my right I heard, "Heeeeeere's Jerome!"

Whatever came out of my mouth wasn't words. A senseless prayer not to be shot. For the impossibility of the Ghost Dance to persist. We danced, and the same whatever it was that we'd felt in Astor, stronger than electricity in the air, it came with us. I felt it prickling my hair, waking up my feet.

Lots of things woke up then. Ghost sort of things. I guess spirits is more accurate because they weren't quite ghosts in the human sense, but elk spirits and salmon. Hawk and beaver and boulder spirits. Water spirits. Dried grass spirits. Mosquito and painted pony and cedar spirits. Grease Trail spirits and Chinook Jargon spirits.

There were Indians, too. Probably from dozens of

different tribes, carrying with them deaths from battle or displacement or disease or misery. I tried but had a hard time recognizing what tribes they all were. There were just too many.

I recognized others; empty bottle and hungry gut and just-scraping-by spirits, no electricity and hand-me-down spirits. Discrimination and no-hope-no-chance spirits. They'd been with us a long time and that's why they came.

All the spirits joined in, dancing the same dance we did but a thousand feet tall, scraping the sky, it seemed like. They pushed aside the roadblock like a river cutting through parched earth and we went on. With that sort of help on our side the city stood no chance.

And that's how we took Creighton; or, how the Ghost Dance proved its name. After meeting in the middle of town we were starving but there wasn't anyplace to eat so we raided a supermarket. Me and the prophet grabbed some chips and pre-wrapped sandwiches and soda, fat slices of German chocolate cake, and sat out on the curb. Listening to the empty city, silent but for the others celebrating in the backs of pickups with radios blasting in a competition of rap and country music. All else was motionless, but for the spirits of our past roaming skyscraper tall among us.

It was hard to stay focused on eating with all those spirits around, and me craning after them like a kid at the zoo. Would they fade with time, or stay? I searched spirit-faces, wondering if Wovoka might be among them.

"He died in Nevada," Mitty said when I thought it out loud.

"So? Maybe his spirit's here."

"In Creighton?"

I shrugged and finished my sandwich.

"So are we gonna do this again?" I asked, as we headed to his car. He could've got a new one but he still stuck to that battered old thing he'd got pulled over in, seemed so long ago now.

"Dunno. Why'd we even do it this time?"

"What do you mean why?"

He leaned against the driver's door. I propped beside him as a sky-tall buffalo spirit ambled over us and past.

"Everyone's gone," Mitty said. "Good and bad didn't make a difference, or rich or poor or anything they thought or did. It was just them and us." He looked away, past the buildings and into the hills beyond. "When Wovoka brought the dance he believed it would fix all our problems. We'd go back to the way we'd been before there were white people."

I looked around. Didn't have to, because I knew what I'd see—guys from school drinking in the backs of their trucks, girls displaying new clothes and cell phones. Everyone taking advantage of the city's bounty that belonged to us now. We weren't have-nots anymore, but what did we have?

Whatever we'd set out to do, it hadn't looked like this in my mind.

"We made our point," I said, trying to sound sure of it. I wondered why Mitty had been the one to find the right steps for the Ghost Dance, and thought I understood. I never should've asked to learn it from him. It wasn't enough to say it belonged to me, to all of us, because that's what had incited Wovoka's dance over a hundred years ago: people hungry to prove they owned things, no matter what it took. Hungry to claim what didn't belong to them simply because they could.

40

"I just want to go home, my feet are killing me," Mitty said, and handed over his keys. I knew he didn't mean Astor but somewhere farther than that, where dusty gray highways led to hills no one would ever fight over. "You drive."

# Ghost Images
by John McCormack

P anix the dog, the space age dog, when he wishes upon a star, he travels in his rocket car," my older brother, Simon, sings when he is asked most questions. Sometimes he gives his imitation of Panix's end of the episode laugh.

Although we live in red dirt stained shack, we have the first television in the county. On the cliff above the company has built a massive transmitter with an antenna that is pointed at our shack. The signal is strong, coming out of our toaster, our heater coils, our teeth, our brains. "It takes lots of transmitter power to cover mountainous terrain," Dad says, quoting the research scientists.

Now that they have given Eisenhower the radar he needed to win the war and modified it to keep high altitude planes hidden over Russia, the company wants to bring television to their homes. They want to be able to sit in their living rooms like people do in pictures in Life or McCall's magazines, and to bask in the schemes of "I Love Lucy," the western escapades or the "Cisco Kid," or the bootlegging evil mobsters of "Dragnet." Like any scientists worth their salt, they need test subjects.

As the massive transmitter spews out an unrelenting loop feed of the Panix cartoon, Dad is required to keep a log of times spent watching plus comments on plot, picture and sound quality. To keep strict scientific standards Dad has no controls. He cannot turn it off, or turn the blaring volume down.

Since Simon is always on our couch, mesmerized by the animated canine, he has taken to writing long, lyrical responses to each viewing of the episode, filling enough pages to keep Dad's employers happy. Right now, the television shows Panix being captured in a riveted metal box that orbits the earth. Our hero is tired, hungry, and

44

without water. Radiation showers upon his cage. "Panix," rings out of his intercom system. It is the accented voice of the professor. "Now that you are my prisoner, I'll have no interference from you or your rocket car."

A weakened Panic replies.. "I'll find a way to stop you, Professor."

"There are no stars for you to wish upon in a metal prison. Soon my atomic cannons will be set up on my lunar base and everyone on earth will be my slave."

After piloting so many bombing runs over Italy, Simon enjoys spending his time being warmed by the murky, gray light and the squeaky voice of a cartoon dog that must defeat a hunchbacked scientist who speaks in a thick Russian accent.

Over the blare of Panix's rocket car exhaust, my father thaws me a TV dinner and tells me that I am as good as anyone because I am getting the same education as the best students in the country. The only reason I am allowed in the company's private school is my father's job. I'm in a class with the colony of rich kids whose parents live below us in white columned houses around Truman Lake.

"Scientific research," Dad says as we pack into his beige Studebaker. He is taken with the idea of scientific research because he sees the lives of the young men that work over him. Even though they are all about the same age as Simon, they didn't have to go to war because they worked in the mountain think tank. Each morning they stuff themselves into tailored suits, fedoras, and shiny shoes, kiss their lipsticked, beehived-haired wives, and climb into their big-finned Cadillacs, steering with hands heavy with diamond rings and stains of imported cigarettes. At work, they drink coffee in florescent lit

45

conference rooms and chat about design efficiencies and signal flow. My dad understands that they are educated and deserve these happy lives.

Each morning, I go to the company with my father. On the top of the mountain, the car radio can get reception from a Memphis radio show. Dad sings along with the Ames Brothers as they harmonize on "Rag Doll." He grows quiet as Doris Day starts vocalizing "Bewitched" before the declining elevation loses the signal in static.

Twenty minutes later, I enter the classroom and join a bunch of boys with oiled hair, clean stretched white shirts, and pressed chinos. They sit at desks, swayed by piles of new textbooks. At the chalkboard scrawls the teacher. He turns around and addresses the group. "Children, we are engaged in a race that will determine the fate of the world, This time it is not war, but exploration, The country that conquers space will control the entire planet," he says then he turns around to write more equations.

As a student in this sixth grade class, I am subjected to this scientist's obsessions. Every day he says that young people should be able to create informative papers. He announces that each evening we are responsible for writing a full page on a science subject that we chose using outside research materials. Wanting to comply with my father's belief in scientific research I look in every inch of the three rooms of our modest home. As much as I try, I cannot write a reasonable paper based on the ingredients listed on the back of a tamale, Mexican rice, and flan TV dinner box. I ask Simon how airplanes work and he talks me through a quick page about the survival rates of low altitude bombing crews.

When my father comes home I tell him my problem.

"I'm going to flunk out of your school because I don't have any research books." I am yelling so I can be heard over the television. Panix is captured by the Professor and is being shot into the sky.

Exhausted from a day of work, irritated by the blasting of the television and now having to face another evening of his children, he asks what research materials I need and I tell him books with stuff in them about science.

"Didn't you get those at school?"

I explain that it is not school work but homework and I need to have research materials. My father frowns then from deep within his weariness beams a smile. He reaches in his pants pocket, counting the small wad of bills that he has in his palm. "Okay," he said, "I think I have an answer." My brother observes Panix's efforts to survive meteorite crash and an end over end spacewalk to signal a falling star.

"There's a dog. She's thirsty," Simon says. "She's far from home, abandoned and confused."

"We know, Simon, Panix, the space dog."

'No," he says. "A real dog. I can see her in the picture's static."

I love getting into the Studebaker and driving down the mountain. Dad plays the radio filling his old sedan with the music of the Andrews Sisters. We sing along with the words of "I Can Dream Can't I" and the first few notes of Nat King Cole's "Mona Lisa" until the sound is drowned in hiss.

Shopping takes place in a sleepy wide spot in the road that has always had a gas station, a bait shop, and a small diner. Now a brand new supermarket is open.

I love to enter the automatic doors of the Family Discount Grocery. The shiny new tile and bright lights thrill me. My

47

father jogs to his destination. He pulls out a stack of TV dinners from the humming, white freezer. "Science," he says to me. He dumps the cold boxes into my arms. "Beans and Franks with cornbread and chopped carrots,' I say. "Spaghetti and meatballs, chopped green beans, and a cherry cake. Turkey slices, mashed potatoes, and candied apples," I add.

"Science," my father says.

My dad walks our cart to a small table, across from the checkout counter. "Look," he says. "Research materials." On the table stands twenty identical volumes. The sign in front of the books says that if a customer buys at least fifteen dollars' worth of groceries, the Family Discount Grocery will sell you the first volume of the Grade School Scholar's Science Encyclopedia for only 49 cents. We soldier through the grocery, my arms burning from holding a pile of frozen dinners, as my father makes me promise I will care for the book, someday taking it to college. He adds the reference book to the icy pile filling my arms

All the way home I glance through my reference book. It covers science topics that begin with the letter "A." Each page has another topic, with accompanying colored drawings. Although, I am attracted to the colors pictures and even the bold type of each entry, I'm not finding a way to translate the encyclopedia words into my paper.

When I get home, I join Simon, on the couch, he's scribbling away at his log book. "Sometimes, I can see her. She's in pain."

"It's just a cartoon, Simon. You need to get away from the house for a while."

"Ghost images," my father says." The scientists said there can be ghost images, buts of broadcasts that bounce off the atmosphere from other signals."

As my father thaws TV dinners, I show Simon my new book. "I've a reference book and I need to write another science paper."

Simon stops his log writing mid-sentence and glances through the book. At the entry for "asteroids," he pauses, slams the book closed and tells me about small planetoids that circle the sun, mostly between the planets. He says there are thousands of asteroids, cosmic leftovers from the parts used to meld into planets. I write down what he says plus add a foreword giving a proper citation for the encyclopedia.

The next morning, my paper is added to the teachers stack of assignment, He speaks to the classroom, as tears flow from his eyes, "Children, you know we have spoken of Sputnik. Our country shamed by not being the first to penetrate space. We have been informed that the Russians have already launched Sputnik II. A Russian spaceship that is sending televised telemetry across the globe." He pauses for a moment, then returns to his subject matter. "Children, if we are to continue to be the America that we have fought a war to continue to be, you must learn what it will take to make outer space American."

That evening Simon tells me that the little dog is sick. He says when he squints he sees her body on the screen. I show him the book and he tells me about 'aerodynamics," "aerodynamics," the study of how to keep things flying in light of the pull gravity. My cover page gives proper credit to my encyclopedia. The third night he skims through the book until he finds an article about the "atmosphere." He explains it allows for wind, makes weather, shields us from the sun, "You know all of those craters on the moon, that's because asteroids crash into its surface, because they don't have an atmosphere, Here on

49

earth, the stuff from the skies just burns up when it gets to the atmosphere. It becomes a fireball, and never hits the surface." My cover sheet notes the page, the editors and the name of the article.

The next evening Simon and I eat dinner, Simon's metal tray holds the meat loaf with catsup gravy, spiced apples, and Brussels sprouts. I'm having the macaroni and cheese, french fries, and cherry cake. I show Simon my book and he sees the word "acceleration." "It's the speed of things. Things going faster and faster. You know we are racing across the sky, twirling around the sun, accelerating all the time."

I am afraid to talk to my father about my paper on the next evening. I don't want him to think that I don't love my reference book. I don't want him to believe that I am ungrateful or have him lose his own happiness in solving what could have been an expensive problem. I don't want him to know that Simon is ghost authoring my papers.

I approach him after our ride home from work "You know that I do enjoy my reference book and it's been just perfect for my papers, but..."

"What's the problem?"

"I promised that I'd take care of the encyclopedia and except for a Coke stain it is in pretty good shape and that wasn't my fault."

"You seem to have taken good care of your book," My father says wanting for me to move this along.

"My teacher wants us to write a research paper using outside materials but he says we have to have more than one source. He says if we do not understand scientific research concepts then the moon will fly a Russian flag."

"One source?" my father asks.

"Look." I explain, my demonstration already organized.

50

"Here's my book. Here's an article about asphyxiation. If I write about this subject I can use this article as only one source. He says I have to have more than one."

"There are lots of pages in your book so lots of things to write about. Can't you..."

"There's only one about asphyxiation. So if write about this topic, I'll need another different book. Don't you see?"

When we arrive at the grocery store, he walks to a table that displays twenty orange books. A sign indicates that the Family Discount Grocery is announcing the sale of the first volume of the High School Encyclopedia of Scientific Knowledge for 49 cents with a purchase of at least fifteen dollars in groceries. I look through the book. It is a thick collection of words and only a few pictures. This is a high school kid's encyclopedia and I feel smart to be seen looking at it.

When we return home, the television is gray and loud. Panix is on the surface of the moon. He leaps over craters. He looks to the sky and his rocket car appears.

Simon tells me about "annihilation." I take notes as he speaks. "Everything must die," While I'm making a cover sheet showing that my paper came from two sources, Simon peers at the screen.

Across the earth, Russian scientists wonder about the fate of a tiny puppy, found in a Moscow alley, that is reentering the atmosphere as a ball of fire.

Simon glances at the reference books entry for "ash." "Bits of solid particulate, left over from a burning or an implosion."

The Panix theme song fills the shack. "Panix the dog, the space age dog" and Simon begins singing along.

Dad and I find the car keys. As we descend, I beat out a

rhythm on the back of the car seat as Dad pounds the steering wheel to the percussive sounds of Perry Como's "Papa Loves Mambo," then the Chordettes begin their harmonious singing of "Mr. Sandman" until the radio signal is lost in the interference.

# You Got Somewhere Better to Be?
## by Linsey Duncan

I 'm glad you aren't trying to convert me," says Jing-Wei to Jane. She phrases it light, like a joke. The two girls walk in the paved lot behind Provo High School, between the main building and the fence that separates the girls from the athletic fields beyond. Seems like every school has a lot like this, a between-place. An empty stretch of nowhere to cross if you want to get to the gym, the cast-off social studies building, the seminary.

Jing-Wei Chou is one of a handful of Chinese exchange students at the school. They get poked and prodded at like the novelties they are. In return for learning the odd bodily proportions of Tomb Raider and other American culture trivia, they must either change to suit their environment or tolerate a childish intolerance of their differences. "You're agnostic, what's agnostic? That's stupid." "Will you come to seminary with me?" "Will you come to seminary with me?"

The targeted differences are mostly religious, after all, oh, naturally. The accents get a few comments, but accents are nothing compared to having a soul purportedly slanted at a different trajectory. Most of the students see themselves walking along the straight and narrow, hanging onto an unseen iron rod. They're young. They're part of a Mormon supermajority. This is a public school with a seminary on-site. This is a public school with a seminary that pressures students to recruit those handfuls of kids who aren't already going.

You're Chinese, good-naturedly polite, unassuming and/or unthreatening in appearance, and you're a target for polite, persistent conversation about maybe, maybe, you'd really like to go to seminary with your classmates. You're Chinese, and completely uninterested in seminaries. Completely uninterested in taking creditless courses slanted toward learning about a particular interpretation of God, Jesus, and Joseph Smith. Uninterested in watching awkwardly acted videos about resisting sin, sin given the form sometimes of a doppleganger or sometimes of a Lamanite, which is a person cursed by God to have darker skin. A person set apart by God so that they are ugly to the righteous ones, the fairer ones, the paler ones. No, soft now, the church does not condone racism and the Book of Mormon has its share of sympathetic Lamanites. Anyone can rise above their curse. Anyone can be worthy of love. All a darker skin means is that you're a little less innately lovable. That your ancestors posed a risk to the faith of the fair ones by their wickedness, their unbelief, their moral sloth. Of course, their sloth.

No, let us be soft again. There are no Chinese people in the Book of Mormon. There are only Jews and American Indians (Africans are left to the Pearl of Great Price, which lightly brushes against that popular seed of Cain, seed of Ham chestnut). There are no just-so stories for the creation of Asians. So there is nothing to fear in these videos. There is nothing about you here. No remonstrance, no sense of having to make up for some distant past, no sense of having some dug-out Godly curse hung over your head. An Asian is just an Asian. So come in, come in. Your skin, if it happens to be a little browner, is no object, not that it ever would've been, God is no respecter of persons except when He is.

But Jing-Wei never comes. It isn't about the skin or the awkward acting, neither of which she ever gets close enough to consider. It's not the fact these supermajorities run in a pack. She has somewhere better to be. She has class scheduled from 7:30 am to 3:00 pm. She has no good reason to wake up two hours early for the extra-school morning session of seminary. When her classmates speak of all the good the church will do for her, when they talk of Holy Spirits and peaceful feelings, it has no meaning. It draws no yearning. This is the difficulty, treating religion as self-help. Jing-Wei is happy and pleasant and has no need for an internal restructuring. Treat the church instead as the one true salvation, no difference. She is agnostic and the promise of a better afterlife is something like the promise of a better undersea kingdom for mermaids. How nice if such things exist, but you don't set up a twenty-year plan to meet the mermaids at the dock.

Jane never asks Jing-Wei to come. The obligation to evangelize is pressed upon her as it is the rest of the supermajority, but it has no real weight. Supermajorities, bless them, have never been monolithic. You might go to seminary between chemistry and English. You might have the Book of Mormon and the Bible stuck in your backpack. You might think it's the best hour of your school day, an hour full of light and truth so intense and wonderful that you're bursting over to share, that you grab the first vaguely Chinese person you see and talk up the blessings of heaven and the blessings of seminary, just come and see. These might be the same yous who will go on a mission in a couple of years, go on missions all over the world, and later say with complete earnestness that it was the best time of their lives. They might not be the same yous.

You might also go because if you don't go to release-time seminary, everyone will know and your parents will know and your bishop will know and God will know, and Jane doesn't want either her parents or God to know that she sits in that chair and passes elaborate notes to her friends and laughs at the videos. But every time she goes,

58

every time she sits, it's like she can feel the walls inside her close in a little bit. There are no videos, in fact,, explicitly about skin color, because this is asking for trouble in a modern church, but there are videos about how if you are a woman and you are very gifted in chemistry, which you happened to just attend . . . anyway, if you are very gifted in chemistry, but also a woman, and your short-sighted female teacher thinks you'd be great, so great at science, and should get an internship or some catastrophic thing like that, the appropriate response is to look off into space and hum to yourself about how a true woman's role first and foremost involves instead the raising and bearing of children.

Jane goes to seminary. She never pulls in Jing-Wei, because despite pressure and prizes of ice cream for those who know how to witness to the point of harassment, because despite feeling on the surface level that perhaps she is going to seminary between chemistry and English because she is a good Mormon and believes in it, because despite everything, she feels the cage inside herself and can't bring herself to take someone pleasant and happy and show them what steel bars look like when you swallow them down one by one.

She keeps going. She goes to the religious university. She learns there that although there is not a just-so story for the creation of Asians, they, too, will rise from the first resurrection purified and white, which is to say, yes, racially white. This is learned in the presence of a darker-skinned Asian, in a room where everyone else is fair and beautiful as per the Book of Mormon, and this is taught in every bit of sweetness and sharingness as seminary was presented. In the end times, you, too, will be white, hallelujah.

She keeps going. The skin color issue is made more

explicit, outside of the confines of a fence that contains both seminaries and public schools. And what about women? Jane learns that only hormonally diseased women play with trucks instead of dolls.

These matters are all the stranger for being so occasional. It isn't every sermon, it isn't every class. You will go to chemistry and English and in between, a surprise, a video, a flyer, an off-remark of a teacher, an off-remark meant to be taken as cultural truth, objective fact, the necessary background to everything you're learning here. Chemistry dies with this life, race is a temporary barrier if you're faithful, and gender is forever.

There's a video Jane saw in seminary, once. Different than the others. Awkwardly acted, through-and-through amateur. Filmed in a seminary bathroom. Theme was skipping seminary is lame, because what else would you be doing? Drawing soap lines in the bathroom, making faces in the mirror.

After all, what better place do you have to be than seminary?

It takes time for Jane to reach down her own throat, extract those bars.

It takes time for Jane to remember that there is happiness outside the bars.

It takes time for Jane to realize, like Jing-Mei, that she does, in fact, have somewhere better to be.

Too much time.

It's years later, years. You have the high school reunions. Yeah, those come and go. You eat cheap catering and see children's movies, because high school reunions must be careful and considerate. Jing-Mei, she's long gone. You aren't going to see her again, any more than you're going to see any of the other people who passed through that school and ended up somewhere other than here, forever.

Jane, she sits on the steps of the high school, waiting for this kid she's supposed to pick up for a friend, a friend who's walked the path everyone's supposed to be walking. Married in the temple, had four kids. Had four kids years ago. Jane, she didn't walk that path. But she didn't walk much of anything. She's drifted from job to job, unemployed occasionally, engaged never. In work, in anything else. Never had a boyfriend, exactly, never a girlfriend, either. Never had a friend she felt sure of. She entertains dreams of becoming great, someday, of unfolding like a butterfly of talent and stunning everyone. Her friends insist she could. Someday. Probably. If she only had the confidence.

She's forty-two. She's not sure she'll ever have the confidence.

Why is she still here? She picks up the kid, takes him home, and keeps driving after that. Drives until she runs out of road, up in the shallows of the mountains.

She pulls off into gravel, slings herself into a crouch, elbows braced on her thighs. She looks down over brown slopes grown-over thin with pale brush.

It's funny. The stuff you internalize. Jane never walked the path set out for her, being born Mormon, but she never exactly got off it either. She walked alongside it, clambering over rocks and dead branches, barking her legs and cutting her feet, not on the path, not actively condoning it, but bizarrely married to it. Like she saw that stupid video about skipping seminary being tantamount to hiding out in the bathroom a few meters away and ripping up paper towels and in all the world, in all of everywhere, she couldn't think of anywhere better to be

61

Linsey Duncan

than a few feet aft of the road she didn't believe in taking.

Oh, you digest those bars. They stay heavy. They root you steps away from where you'd be otherwise, if you hadn't rebelled your tiny rebellion. You don't really practice the faith you were raised in, it's empty to you, has been forever. But you never make the choice to find happiness apart from it. You hide in the proverbial bathroom and you never come out.

Jane, she takes a deep breath, and she tells the scrub and the loneliness, "I'm going."

But even if Jane's somewhere to be is a rented room in a basement in the middle of North Dakota, it's a somewhere chosen.

And that's a start.

# The Devil's Details
by Amberle L. Husbands

O n paper, it was one thing, and around the water cooler the back office was affectionately known as the Bait Shop. In reality, it was a closet encasing a bank of computers, an assortment of cameras, speakers, two chairs, and Lola.

Martin liked to get to the office early, before the huge influx of his coworkers arrived at eight o'clock. The place was nicer, he thought, when it was empty. He liked the feeling of leaving his wife at home, asleep, and going through the sleeping streets, and then showing up to a mostly slumbering building. In the civil service manufacturing room, eleven policemen and two meter-maids awaited the final airbrushing on their new skins, awake and staring out, looking like a stag party gone terribly wrong. In research and development, the two newest prototypes sat facing one another over a chess board, in front of a camera, ready to set-to each other when some intern came in to hit their switches. The game would probably be done with in under three minutes, but there would be other tests, too; only one new model would be released in the fall, and both parental design teams knew it.

He by-passed the break-room, watching the brown smudgy reflections of himself in the plate glass walls. As usual, there were already a few other early-risers gathered there, blowing on their coffee and shaking their heads over the concept of Mondays.

"—ain't like Frank made it..."

The words were only a high spike in the general grumbling, but they caught Martin's attention briefly. Frank had been in the custom of making break-room coffee, first thing every morning. He'd been an even earlier bird than Martin liked to be. Three weeks ago, Frank had been found in his garage, dead in his car of asphyxiation.

He'd had a pistol in his lap, loaded, just in case there wasn't enough gas in the tank to finish the job. But there'd been plenty of gas; the engine was still running when the fire department showed up. It was simple and clean, done with in a matter of hours, and the city had burned Frank to ashes. Simple and clean.

But Frank hadn't had a wife at home, Martin thought. But he forgot it as soon as the break-room's glint faded behind him.

In the bait-shop, Lola sat at her terminal. Her head was slumped down over her thin chest, and her cropped copper hair swung forward to hide her face. Each freckle across her shoulders and the back of her neck was strategically places, each golden glint in her hair was perfectly planned. Martin knew that there was someone in the development department—Burt Steiter, perhaps—who had numbered the hairs on her head. They'd decided the optimal height; her feet hovered a good nine inches off of the floor and their toenails were painted bubblegum pink. The Devil was in the details, Martin thought, trying not to let his gaze linger on those airbrushed toes.

He closed the office door and hung his tweed jacket over he back of the room's empty chair. It was barely forty degrees out in the street, but Lola sat slumped in her denim short-shorts and lilac cotton camisole, same as always.

Martin reached out and ran two fingers beneath one of the camisole's straps, looking down on the thin, freckled shoulder. He studiously tried to avoid contact with the skin.

"We're going to have to get you a few more outfits, Lola," he mumbled. "People are going to get suspicious, otherwise."

67

Nothing answered him.

With a Monday morning sigh, Martin turned and put coffee into the little two-cup machine, reaching for the paper sack with powdered cream and sweetener and paper cups as he switched it on. He took a bottle of Rolaids out of his coat pocket, and sat them beside the machine. With the coffee brewing, he began powering up the computers that ringed three walls of the office. The fourth wall was hung with magazine clippings of shirtless pop heart-throbs and a techno-coloured unicorn poster. The Devil's details once again.

Finally, when the room buzzed with power, Martin sat down in his swivel chair. He reached out and turned Lola around to face him, her body swaying loosely with the motion of the chair, and took up her right wrist like a man looking for someone's pulse. He pressed inward, gently.

Suddenly, there was a heatless life coursing through the fingers in his grip. Lola's face tilted up, as open and expressionless as any child's upon first awakening. Then, she smiled.

"Good morning, Martin."

"Morning, Lola."

Martin held her hand a moment longer, watching her face. "Did you sleep well?"

"Yeah," she nodded, affectionate and irreverent. One of her bare feet swung gently, kicking out its little pink toes. "The bus woke me up again, blowing its stupid old horn. But, I'm sick of school."

Martin nodded absently, letting her hand drop. It was part of the script; there was no bus, and no school, but there were men all over the world, some just waking up and some who'd been eating dinner, who thought that

68

there was a bus and a school. Lola smiled impishly at Martin, for all the world—he thought—as if she understood the difference between the act and reality.

All act, he told himself firmly, fixing a cup of coffee. It's all an act, there is no damned reality on this side of that office door.

He threw away the red plastic stirrer and shook two Rolaids out into his palm.

"Ready to get to work, then?"

•

It was forty minutes later before the first bite came in.

Martin was on his third cup of coffee, and was losing miserably to Lola at black jack. It was the only card game he even stood a chance of matching her at, and even on his luckiest days it felt like a loser's endeavor. He kept half an eye on the computer monitors, feeling at a disadvantage; Lola could play cards and monitor everything without even expending extra effort. Every few seconds one of the screens would show a message she had sent—through that enviable electronic telepathy of hers, Martin thought—to one of the three dozen conversations she was currently involved in. A delay had been programmed in to simulate a slightly slower-than-average typing speed for the ten year old girl she was supposed to be.

Lola turned over a seven, and her head snapped up, copper hair swinging.

"Bigman221 wants to start a video session."

Martin laid his cards down and wheeled into the room's blind spot, turning to his own computer, the Nanny. The conversation she referred to came floating to the front with a few keystrokes; Martin scanned the lines, then nodded to Lola. He sighed quietly to himself and reached for another antacid.

She manually pulled herself up to the desk, and Martin watched her flip her hair almost like a little human girl before turning on the camera.

"Hi there, that's better," the speakers spat out a man's voice—Bigman221's voice—that could have been the voice of any English-speaking man in the world. "Yeah you're right, it is a little bit shorter than my daughter's. And red, too. I like that."

Martin listened impassively, scanning the previous exchanges to catch up on the conversation Bigman was continuing. Lola smiled haughtily and shook her head.

"My step-dad likes it, too, but Mom says that it makes me wild."

"Well, you're talking to me, aren't you?" Bigman sat back away from his camera, and Martin saw that it was dusk out the windows above and behind his head. Lola giggled convincingly.

"You ever do shows?" Bigman asked, resting one hand on the bulging round of his stomach. "I can pay, you know."

The conversation before had been the usual material, Martin saw; how old are you, are you in school, do you like older men, have you done this or that before... It was pretty tame, compared to some of the stuff they got. This guy, as it happened, had triggered Lola's good-girl-gone-rebellious personality; what they affectionately called the Red-headed-step-child persona. Martin shuddered to think about what came out of her, whenever she got on with the really weird ones.

Lola looked down at her lap and then away, biting her bottom lip deliberately. Then, she shrugged, unsmiling.

70

"Thirty dollars."

"I'll do twenty." Bigman had dropped his smile too. "For fifteen minutes. Naked."

Lola shrugged, still looking away, and pulled her shoulders forward self-consciously. Martin was always worried that the men would back out at her seeming reticence.

"Twenty-five. Come on, I'm horny."

But they never did.

"Okay," Lola said soberly, sitting up straighter. "Have you done this before?"

"Yeah, yeah, I know the drill."

Martin felt his skin begin to crawl. This was something he never quite built up a tolerance for. Lola, of course, took it in stride. She even sat back in her chair, throwing one foot up onto the edge of the desk beside her keyboard.

"Go ahead, kid, take off your top. I got the money."

Martin shivered, keeping his eyes glued to his own screen and the image of Bigman221 that festered there. He slipped a Rolaid into his mouth and crunched it silently, sucking on the chalky tablet. But he could still hear Lola, her shirt hitting the floor, her giggles. He could still see the tips of her bubble-gum pink toenails, out of the corner of his eye. He shifted a styrofoam coffee cup around on his knee, hoping they wouldn't get any of the really weird ones for a while.

•

"I need some new clothes."

Martin looked up sharply at Lola, wondering how much of the environment she remained sensible to, during her shutdowns. Could she have heard him, earlier?

71

Could she have heard him say other things, other times?

"Maybe one of those Pink Point shirts," she continued, swinging one foot back and forth. The other was curled beneath her in the chair. The little twitches and bored animations—the swinging leg, or the drumming fingers—were strokes of genius on the part of the design team.

Martin shook his head. "No, those cover up too much... But you do need new clothes."

"They're the thing, now," she insisted, and Martin thought he almost heard a pre-teen whine in her voice. "Every girl should have one; the ad says so."

"Come on, you're too smart for that... But I'll talk to the profilers. It doesn't matter what every girl has, really, it just matters what every man wants."

Lola shrugged. "They want me."

Martin couldn't think of an answer.

Sometimes, when she got smart or used her almost-whining voice, Martin wondered if she was playing a persona crafted especially for him. Did she differentiate between her handler and the men on the internet? Or was it all part of an inner-office ploy to get him terminated? After all, it was a cozy little job, sitting down and acting as the invisible Nanny all day, drinking coffee, playing cards with an android. There were plenty of people who would gladly sit in the closet all day, taking the time to work on their graduate papers, or whatever it was they wanted spare time to do. Burt from development, for instance. He'd been one of the ones working on Lola, to begin with. He would jump at the chance to study her in depth, in action.

Maybe it was a trap, Martin thought. Maybe he was a lab-rat.

But maybe it wasn't. Maybe the persona she turned on

him was one of her own decisions. Wasn't she supposed to absorb and adapt? When she looked at him from beneath the copper fringe of her hair, for instance, or when she bent to examine the airbrushing on her toes in such a precious little-girl way—those had to be acts for his benefit. Didn't they?

When she pinned him down with those crystalline, amber eyes...

When she played with the straps on her camisole, back and forth, back and forth...

"Isn't your shift over, Martin?" She nodded towards the bank of computers. "We're not that busy, right now. Just three that we already have files on."

Martin sighed and stood up, stretching backward to unzip his spine. The office chairs were ergonomic like a bed of nails would have been. He reached mechanically for an antacid tab, shook one out, and put the bottle back in his pocket.

"Guess it is. Alright, sign off then."

With the typing-speed delay, it took her about twenty seconds. The monitors all went blank, and the low hum of the room began to die off by degrees. Lola turned from the desk to offer him a generic, basic-programming smile.

"Goodnight, Martin," she chirped, just before sighing and letting her head slump down again, hair swinging forward, her toes hanging motionless nine inches above the carpet. Martin paused for a minute, staring down at her. He put his coat on, feeling the stiffness in his shoulders from sitting down all day. Then, he leaned down to kiss the sleek crown of her copper-coloured hair.

"Goodnight, Lola... you beautiful little whore."

•

Matilda talked in her sleep, as Martin waited for his alarm clock to go off. The rifling of her dreaming brain should have made him feel less alone, but it didn't. The clock went off, and he reached out to silence it.

Tuesdays were reserved for the really weird ones. After months and months, Martin felt sure there was some unwritten, universal scheme that ordained it so. Maybe God got bored on Tuesdays. Or maybe, Martin thought, God and the antacid companies had come to some mutually beneficent agreement about Tuesdays.

He desperately wanted the current act to end so that he could turn the coffee pot back on, to brew another two cups that might get him through the last hour of the shift. But the hissing, gurgling machine would be out-of-place in a ten-year-old girl's bedroom.

The current act—a typical Tuesday scenario—had brought out Lola's darkest persona; the over-achieving-but-fallen prodigal daughter, abuse victim turned nymphomaniac. The bright, jaded bruise of a girl, hungering for some fresh kind of pain.

Tuesdays were full of men who had just invented all kinds of new pains.

Just the sounds were enough to drive a man insane. The articulations, the verbal exchanges... Mr. Psych-9er's fifteen minutes of screen time couldn't end soon enough to suit Martin. When it finally was over, Martin swallowed back the sourness that coated his teeth and flicked on the coffee maker, scowling at it. But it jumped into action as cheerfully as ever, blinking its delight at being allowed to bubble hot water through old coffee grounds for him.

"We almost have everything on him," Lola chirped, after separating her generic persona from the freak she'd been just minutes before. "That one's file will be full, soon."

Martin pressed two antacid tablets between his right molars and crushed them mechanically. He could feel anger and disgust grating against each other in the pit of his stomach.

"We shouldn't have them speaking to you that way."

Lola blinked to refocus her eyes, leaving the mental folder she'd been rifling through. "The point of the Project is to identify and track criminals, Martin. This is the way they speak to me, and the way I speak to them. The profilers have found—"

"Right, right, I know what the profilers have found..."

Martin grimaced and threw hot, weak coffee down his throat to wash away the last of the chalk dust. He knew he would vomit, if he tried to eat anything when he got home that night, and that would depress Matilda. There wasn't anything he could do about that.

He looked up at Lola, who hadn't moved from her chair. She'd even stopped swinging her leg, staring at him.

"It's natural to be disturbed, Martin," she said. "The Program is—"

"Disturbing, I know. Believe me, I know."

She sat there, looking at him with her glass eyes, with perfect little lines of sympathy tucked into her forehead. Calculated signs of human emotion. Martin waited for the next string of calculations, of statistical odds, to pour out of her mouth.

"It's okay, Martin," she said. Lola quickly leaned forward, to put a hand on his knee. "It's okay to be disturbed."

The knock at the door made Martin jump, and Lola moved like lighting to catch the coffee cup before it was bounced off the desk's surface.

"It's okay," Martin called, hearing himself parroting the robot but with a slight tremor in his voice. "We're not live, come on in."

The door popped open and Burt Steiter thrust his orange-tanned face into the room. He looked first to Lola, and then to Martin as an afterthought.

"Teaching her to drink coffee now, Marty?" He smiled too widely. "Just had to pass on your bad habits didn't you? Can't stand a creature born perfect, can you? Hey, you hear about Gomez?"

"Huh? What about him?"

"He checked himself into the psych ward Sunday night. Just put his driver's license on the front desk and said 'help me'. Shipped his daughter off to live with family upstate."

"That's, uhm... yeah. Did you need something, Burt?"

The man came the rest of the way into the room, scanning the activity on the computers possessively. "I need to start getting all the data presentable. We only have another two weeks, after all, and everything needs to be neat and tidy by the Project's end. Gonna have to steal Lola from you for a little while, Marty."

"Right, uhm—" Martin stood up too fast, got dizzy, and caught himself on the arm of his swivel chair. "Of course. I clock out in twenty minutes, anyway. Go ahead, we're at a good slow spot, and she can shut everything down on her own from this point... I'm the expendable one here, anyway."

•

It was a wild scheme—the kind that aren't even born in proper dreams but only surface out of that murky, head-ache

76

riddled backwash between dreaming and coming awake. But the longer it sat in his head, the more sense if made.

Martin turned the idea over every few seconds, while scrambling eggs in his dingy galley kitchen; he wanted bacon, but lately his stomach couldn't handle it. He thought about it again while showering, while masturbating, while combing his hair, while putting together a suit from the pile of clothes on his bedroom floor... And slowly the hazy dream-logic wore off and a lucid core began to peak through, like a stone being polished until it glittered.

He didn't have the luxuries of other men; he couldn't afford to die, couldn't even afford to have a nervous breakdown. And he didn't have any family up-state.

But as his front door clicked shut behind him, leaving him at the mercy of another gray, wet winter morning, he realized dimly that a wild scheme just might work. He also realized, just as dimly, that he would try it regardless. He stopped into the thrift store two blocks up from his own grimy apartment, making quick and calculated selections so as not to be late for work.

But he was still there before most of the day shift. There was only one android slumped over the chess board, now, in research and development. The dead-faced stag party had been broken up.

Martin made coffee before waking Lola up, guiltily anticipating the little flutter in her fingers as he pressed her wrist, and the blank, energetic smile she greeted him with each day.

"Good morning, Martin."

"Morning, Lola... Did you sleep well?"

"Yeah. The bus woke me up again, blowing its stupid old horn. But, I'm sick of school."

How'd you like to go out, instead? Martin almost gave himself away, then, but he wanted to test the waters first. There was still the possibility that she was his trap, too, and that the minute he stepped wrong they would come down on him.

"Well, let's get to it," he said, trying to sound as he did every morning.

All of the computers flashed on at once and began buzzing, but Lola didn't turn towards them. She didn't even blink when they came alive. "What's in the bag, Martin?"

"Oh, those new clothes we talked about. Here, see what you think." He fished around in the paper sack until he came up with the new tank-top, and held it out to her.

She smiled gently. "I won't look as good in purple, Martin. The colour wheel—"

"But plenty of girls are into purple, this year. I saw it in, uh... you know, that catalog thing..."

"It's the fourth most popular scheme of the season," Lola said immediately. "Purple and gold. The biggest are blue and beige, green and pink, yellow—"

"I think you'll look just fine in it, Lola."

She shrugged. "What else?"

Martin pulled out all of the camisoles and shorts, and then—hesitantly—the multicolored knit skirt. Then he rolled the top of the bag back down and tossed it quickly beneath his side of their shared desk, handing her clothes.

She analyzed them instantly, only pausing a second to take stock of the skirt. "Those will do. Should I change now?"

Martin swallowed.

"That's up to you, Lola... Are there any bites yet?"

78

•

"Well that one was fun."

The most disturbing part, Martin thought, was the minute or so it took for Lola to come out of her chosen persona after an encounter was finished. Especially after she finished with one of the really weird ones.

"That one wasn't in our system, yet," she chirped, sounding definitely upbeat, possibly even pleased, exhilarated... She pulled the purple tank top back down over her head.

"They get more inventive every day," Martin sighed. He poured himself some coffee and mixed in a lot of creamer, realizing he was out of Rolaids. Inside, he was shaking with hate of the men whose false names and faces appeared on the screens, whose voices came over the speakers to fill his head with filth... But he was also trembling with excitement. To hell with testing the waters, he thought.

Lola seemed to take a breath, and the next thing Martin knew she was her blank-faced, innocent ten-year-old self again; the freak was gone. "Are we done for the day then, Martin?"

"I think so, Lola, yes." His hand shook as he held the coffee to his lips, and Lola went through her signing off procedures.

When she had finished, he thought he saw her pause, to run the tips of her fingers across the knit fabric of the new skirt that covered her lap... but that was probably just his imagination. She turned to him and smiled her customary good-night smile.

"Lola, are the cameras off?"

She blinked, perhaps having to take a second to backtrack on the uncustomary command question. "Yes,

Martin. The cameras are off."

"And the computers, too? Off altogether?"

"Yes," she nodded, her face a lovely blank. The design team hadn't even skimped on the freckles across her cheeks. He wished they had given her the ability to blush.

"Lola, let's get out of here."

"Excuse me, sir?"

That checked him. To the best of his knowledge, she had never called him 'sir' since the day he accepted the Bait Shop job. He took a deep breath, knowing she was simply asking for clarification of an order.

"I want you to change clothes again," he said, taking up the paper bag. This time he took out a baggy fisherman's sweater, a pair of acid washed blue jeans, a slate gray beanie, and a pair of clunky black boots. The ugliest outfit he could conceive of.

As far as he knew, no-one had ever brought her shoes before. They were not one of the Devil's necessary details. He'd guessed at her size—having spent enough time, heaven knew, staring at her little bare feet—and two pairs of extra thick wool socks, just in case he was wrong.

"Put these on, Lola."

She took them from him, but only held the garments in her lap.

"Martin, I don't think these will be effective. Research shows that men—"

"I know what the research says. You don't need to be pretty, for this. Just put on those cloths."

Another blink. Then, she stood up and pulled the camisole off over her head. Martin turned away. Belatedly, he scanned the corners the room's ceiling for anything that could have been a camera. But the Bait Shop really was nothing more than a glorified supply closet, decked out in little-girl gear on one wall.

"Listen, once you're dressed, we're going to leave this room. You're going to follow me down the hallway and through the lobby with your head down. We're not going to hold hands, and you're not going to say anything to anyone. I'll give you a clipboard to hold, and a cup of coffee—nobody will say anything to you, either. You'll look like an intern. And then we're going to leave the building. And when we get out the doors... we'll just keep going."

"Martin? I don't understand—"

"You don't need to understand, you just need to get dressed."

"But... these strings..."

He turned back around, to find her seated on the floor in the jeans and sweater and socks, with the shoes on her feet, holding both laces of one shoe in her left hand, both of the other in her right. Even in the world's most hideous clothing, she was beautiful. Martin would have laughed, if his stomach hadn't been in knots. With all of her absorbed research and data, her meticulous programming, fashion-trend matrices and all, she couldn't tie a shoe lace. Martin felt something in his chest swell almost to bursting.

"Let me," he said. "But watch closely. It's easy enough—"

He did the first one, and she followed his motions with the other one a second's delay behind him.

Five minutes later, they had almost made it out. Martin glanced at their reflections in passing, caught on the glass walls of the manufacturing bay. Lola was performing admirably, walking with her head bent over the clipboard on the crook of one arm, coffee cup steaming untouched in her other hand. She stayed five or six paces behind Martin, like just another employee making their way to the street. He had schooled her in the bait shop, wondering if she would follow orders once outside that environment.

But why wouldn't she, he thought. That's all she does. That's her life. One big script to follow through, day after day.

Still, sometimes he wondered.

"Martin, hey!"

A hand clapped down on Martin's shoulder like a deadbolt being thrown home. He turned around, stopped in his tracks, and found the bearded, spray-tanned, trendy face of Burt Steiter beaming down on him. Burt from development. Burt the envious entrapment man. Martin felt himself pinned down beneath the man's glowing smile, like a slice of fluorescent lighting. Just out of the corner of his eye, he saw Lola pass by them, her copper hair just visible beneath the dingy beanie. Even in disguise, she gleamed like a beacon; Martin had no idea how no-one noticed the shooting star cutting straight through their crowd.

What had been his order to her?

"Just wanted to make sure you guys have all the reports done by the Project's end, Marty," Burt prattled, still holding him hostage. "You know it's gonna be a whirlpool for entrapment suits, if we don't get our end right, and—"

Martin nodded, deaf and mute. His stomach churned and his eyes remained locked with Burt's, but his mind was traveling out the back of his skull, across the lobby, towards the glass doors, trying to follow, looking around frantically for a glimmer of copper... What had been the exact words he'd spoken to Lola? The words were important. The precise words, the precise direction... A pair of iron hands were squeezing off his lungs... What had he told her to do?

Just keep going.

He'd said they would just keep going.

Would she fail to follow orders? Would she walk out into traffic, and let things end in that ridiculous, haphazard way? Or would she keep going, day after day, and disappear altogether? He might never find her. It might be the end of their story, anyway.

Martin could feel the sweat beginning to stand out on his forehead. His chest filled with pain, cutting him in two. "Burt, I've got to go, now—"

"Not coming down with something, are you?" Burt's eyebrows squeezed together in a mockery of compassion. "I've got a great old flu remedy, completely natural. Let me—"

"I've got to go, Burt."

Martin wrenched his shoulder away and hurried, hunched over and grim, towards the glass doors. He couldn't let things end in an unexplainable traffic accident, or a simple, unreported disappearance. He couldn't... He didn't know how they could live, or if he could or would be happy... but he knew he was soon to find out.

Martin hit the doors, unable to take another breath. Skyscrapers rose up all around, filtering the sun at weird angles, and taxis hissed by. Fresh air teased his face.

His heart—

Across the street, a group of schoolgirls trudged onward, their bright galoshes shattering the sidewalk puddles. Lola looked back over her shoulder once, amber eyes flashing, as she joined the crowd.

Martin fell to his knees as she turned and walked away.

# Among the Aspens
by Alicia Cole

The desks range around April in perfect rows. No lunch today. In the classroom it is quiet.

Sun stains the bulletin board, decorated to show the warming weather outside. Daffodils. Tulips. April often counts the petals.

A buzz of noise in the hallway. Richaud saunters into the classroom followed by Tanya. Sliding into the seat behind her, she begins to braid April's hair.

May arrives next, then Finnegan and Cooper. Like he does every day, Cooper pulls the door shut behind him while the rest of the student body explodes out of the cafeteria. Raucous laughter. A few hand slaps on their classroom door. A quick cry of, "Retards!"

April hears their teacher first, her authoritative, "Move it."

The after-lunch bell sounds its alarm and Mrs. Lewis enters the room.

She gives Tanya and April a disapproving look. "No hair braiding, ladies, that's for recess."

Tanya leans back.

Finnegan makes a quick shot at the wastebasket while Mrs. Lewis is distracted. His paper ball hits the rim and bounces to the floor. The room falls still.

Slumping, Finnegan retrieves the paper and tosses it into the trash, avoiding Mrs. Lewis' gaze.

She smiles. "Better shot next time, Finn." She scans the room then, expression serious, "But before the last bell!"

Finnegan straightens his shoulders and tosses Mrs. Lewis a thankful smile. He might not earn detention today.

·

April studies the board. The lesson, etched out in

marker, lists numbers and formulas. Math is the hardest part of the day.

She flips her card to yellow and Mrs. Lewis nods. The message: she'll need guided support to complete this lesson.

While April waits, the numbers at the top of the board, the date, begin to jiggle and straighten. The month and year sprout leaves while the day lengthens, forming a trunk speckled with the black of marker and the white of the board.

Leaves rampage over the top of the board. Behind one, a furtive creature, squirrel-like with a rounded face and stubby tail, smiles.

"April?"

Mrs. Lewis draws April's attention back to her own miniature white board on her desk. "Try this problem for me. Let's go through our steps, okay?"

$2X = 24$

April's mouth furrows while Mrs. Lewis prompts April to write her list.

"First, isolate the variable."

"Get the letter by itself," April translates, her voice quiet and hesitant. She writes her translated note on her board.

April stops, her stomach cramped with anxiety. She flips her card to red.

"Opposite operations," Mrs. Lewis continues in a calm tone. "How are the 2 and the X connected? What's invisible between them?"

April makes a swift dot on her board between the number and the variable: $2*X = 24$.

"Good, exactly."

A chitter erupts from the whiteboard at the front of the class. April starts. Mrs. Lewis, on her haunches by April's

87

desk, smiles. "What operation is that? Pick out the word for me, April."

April stands and ignores the rustling creature on the board. She points to the word *multiplication* on the word wall.

Before she can return to her seat, Mrs. Lewis asks, "What's the opposite of multiplication?"

April jabs her finger at *division*, notices her teacher's approval, and returns to her seat.

There is a shuffling noise, like furred feet moving through underbrush, as she sits.

"Before you go on," Mrs. Lewis prompts, pointing to the list on the side of April's board, "Finish your steps."

April makes three careful notes: do the opposite operation, the opposite of multiplication is division, complete the problem.

After she finishes the computation, earning a smile and a "Well done" from Mrs. Lewis, April pulls out her math notebook to copy down the steps for that night's homework.

She feels the brush of whiskers on her cheek and jumps.

Tanya pokes her in the back. "Math got you nervous?"

April smiles and holds her right thumb and forefinger up, close together. *A little bit.*

•

During English, when the words swirl around her head with their tornado of meaning, April watches a second creature appear from behind the marker aspen's trunk.

It hops across the board, rabbit-like, indicating the correct word.

She keeps her card at green. English is an easy subject.

88

·

Science is more problematic. The aspen creatures have overrun the white board, but no one else seems to notice.

Richaud's hand shoots into the air question after question, rattling off correct answers. Ann seconds him, eager if less certain. Today's topic: classification.

Finnegan is sent to the principal's office for falling asleep twice.

Tanya gets in trouble for sneaking a piece of gum.

Cooper and April both sit, quiet.

"How should we be classified?" a feathery voice whispers in April's ear.

Her brow wrinkles in concentration. She studies the notes on the board, what she can see peeking out from the leaves. On her desk, a worksheet instructs her to categorize organisms based on traits.

The squirrel-like creature is marked in one category: small land mammals with tails.

The rabbit-like creature hunches to one side, uncertain. Should it go with the squirrel?

The feathery bird is placed in a category all its own. Scaled organisms slither across the base of the board. They also earn their own category.

The rabbit finally joins the squirrel.

April switches her card to yellow and jabs her hand in the air. Cooper's mouth makes a surprised 'o' shape at her gesture while he struggles to complete his worksheet.

Mrs. Lewis approaches. April forms her words. "Can you..." she pauses, flips her math notebook open to jab at the word 'divide', then she points at 'squirrel' and 'rabbit.'

Her teacher beams. "Yes, you can! Let's try something, April. Let me see your white board and marker."

Mrs. Lewis writes squirrel and rabbit at the top of the board and draws a line down the middle. "Write as many traits as you can think of for each organism, then call me back."

•

Birds with long, curled beaks and marvelous, furred tails dance along the side of her board. A few aspen leaves dot the left hand corner. Strange animals cavort around the classroom as April decides on their similarities and differences.

Cooper gives up on the worksheet and is given an earlier lesson to review. Ann and Tanya earn independent reading time.

Richaud works on his own self-guided project while Finnegan, returned from the principal's office, completes the assignment with Mrs. Lewis' re-teaching.

April lists the two animals' traits and, with guidance, makes a Venn diagram. By the end of the day, she is certain: the squirrel and the rabbit belong in different categories, their traits being too dissimilar.

•

The hallway that afternoon is a new world. April categorizes students by eye shape, hair color, body type. She moves, unnoticed as usual, taking in all the details.

Similarities. Differences.

A wing flutters every so often behind her ear, encouraging her when the categorization becomes difficult, pointing out the subtle differences April misses.

At home, she shows her mother how to categorize items in the messy desk drawer. Then, holding her thumb up for 'same', down for 'different', she points out their shared features: nose, hair line, chin. Her mother laughs.

"Can we try your father also?"

Comparing three people at once proves difficult for April and she gives up, not with her usual tantrum—tears and frustrated stomping—but a resigned shrug. Her father kisses her forehead.

"You did very well with your mom and yourself, okay?"

April grins, pleased.

In her room, later, she makes a nest from socks and shredded tissue for the winged creature that has followed her home.

It sleeps there overnight.

•

The next day during Science, Mrs. Lewis seats April with Cooper. They are given a review worksheet to complete together.

"I don't understand," he admits to her, looking up at her then down. April laughs and pulls out her pencil pouch.

She dumps the contents on their desks, pushed together for the lesson review. April arranges three pencils parallel to each other and gives Cooper a thumbs-up. Then, she adds a blue pen to the set.

He grabs it with a too-loud, "No!"

Tanya glances up, distracted from her work with Richaud. "What're you two doing?"

Cooper blushes, then tells April, voice lowering, "They don't fit. Like this." He places two blue pens together.

April nods, says, "More."

Grasping the concept, Cooper groups the different items dumped from April's pouch. When they answer the last question on their worksheet, Cooper high fives April.

•

The aspen creatures appear again during Math. They make faces at her from the board when she sighs, frustrated.

Cooper sounds a sharp, "Whoah!"

"Cooper?"

"Sorry, Mrs. Lewis! I get it," he says.

April notices a squirrel head, miniature with tufted ears and an un-squirrel-like face peeking at her from Cooper's left hand.

He doesn't respond, even though it stretches.

With difficulty, April focuses on the lesson: variable equations resulting in mixed numbers.

Distracted and faced with a difficult lesson, April becomes unresponsive. She keeps her card at red.

Mrs. Lewis is unsuccessful with the algebra tiles. April ends the day slumped over at her desk.

She doesn't notice Cooper watching her.

•

That night, Cooper's mother calls her mother to ask if they might work together on their homework.

April perks up a bit. Her father, having just wrestled the red pen from her which she's slashed in frustration across one page of her math notebook, nods at her mother's query.

"They can work here at the table."

•

It's slow going, Cooper explaining the math lesson while April labors to produce what's needed. Still, she responds better to him than to her parents and they laugh as they work.

Her mother watches from the kitchen.

April's non-verbal explanation of science goes over well.

When Cooper's mother returns to pick him up, their parents talk. April hears: they can meet for homework again next Monday.

•

The weekend seems very long to April.

Her bird-creature busies itself fancying its nest, stealing strings and bits of jewelry from around the room. It squawks in annoyance when April retrieves a pair of earrings.

She wears these at the kitchen table on Monday evening.

This time, the squirrel-creature appears with Cooper. April giggles at it, perched on top of Cooper's head. He giggles back, but doesn't notice when it yawns. Her parents do not notice, nor do they notice the strange feathered rustling in April's hair, the sharp beak that keeps nibbling at her earring back trying to remove it.

In the midst of listing the characteristics of fish, she swats at her left ear. Cooper falls out of his chair, laughing.

•

At school April notices the leaves crinkle and brown, the wind from an open window winnowing them across the white board and depositing their detritus into the marker holder. Fewer creatures roam the room than in previous weeks. Her contented bird snuggles against her neck. When Mrs. Lewis talks, it sings. With each trill, a strip of bark falls.

Soon after she and Cooper begin to hold hands in the hallway, his squirrel disappears into a bank of lockers. A few aspen leaves, brittle and old, litter the ground.

Cooper squeezes April's hand in his.

To her pleasure, her creature shows no sign of leaving. When they complete their homework together twice a week, April's bird-like animal perches on her shoulder.

Her mother peeks her head out from the kitchen. Cooper waves.

•

On her sixteenth birthday, after they've sung happy birthday in the classroom, her bird-creature hops from her shoulder and alights on the window sill. It taps its beak three times and the window creaks open. The fallen leaves are composted on the ground, the branches broken in heaps.

April gestures at it, ignoring Mrs. Lewis' frown.

"You're excited about your birthday, aren't you, April?" she asks, closing the window.

When she looks at Cooper smiling, she doesn't feel like crying anymore.

The final leaves fall from the board and disappear.

Cooper still talks more than she does. Tanya giggles and makes kissy-faces at them in the classroom. Math remains a struggle, but April eats lunch in the cafeteria more often among the noise of French fries being eaten, arguments and laughter.

# Night Birds
by Adele Gardner

Everything seemed sharper in 1983, the year I turned fifteen. October descended with the sudden shock of cold water. Summer faded into fall overnight, and the ground felt crisp as I waited for the bus in a dimness too blue to be called dawn. Trees flamed with an ethereal beauty where the sun touched their tips.

When we'd moved to Kentucky two years ago, there weren't many opportunities to make friends. Our streets held mostly elderly neighbors. At school, cliques formed at birth, based on wealth. After a long period in which Dad had been laid off, my parents still had back-breaking debts, and our clothes were obvious cast-offs.

Erich Brach was one of a handful of other outsiders; like me, he came from a family of transients, though his father was a colonel and mine a civil servant. Erich looked like a World War I flying ace, a checkered scarf flung jauntily over his bomber jacket. I could spot Erich by his scarf and flaming hair across the gym, the hall, the library. His patrician nose, cleft chin, and deep blue eyes marked him the handsomest boy in our class. He had a crooked smile that melted the hearts of the girls in our grade—and mine.

When school started that year, I'd sent Erich an anonymous love letter. He hadn't answered. When I saw him trading sarcastic jokes with football players or being teased by cheerleaders, I feared he'd start to shun me. Then he'd lean over in English and whisper sarcastic jokes in a camaraderie that showed he either didn't know I'd sent the letter, or did not care.

A week before Halloween, Erich persuaded my mom to drop us at the carnival, since he'd pay. Pumpkin lanterns swung in the night wind, casting an orange glow across the blacktop. The light didn't reach the dark spaces between the rides, or the pitch inside the tent where a young girl turned ape, rearing to tear us limb from limb. Scarecrows and zombies rose from fall sheaves; figures in leotard-black with mime-white faces leapt from the shadows. I almost jumped out of my skin. We ran, laughing.

"Maneater" and "Thriller" piped over the speakers. Dying leaves skittered along the blacktop, while red and orange garlands draped the stalls. Racks of prizes advertised games of skill and chance.

Erich smiled. "Hey, Hal, let's try a game of skill. My brawn against your brains. Or is it the other way round?"

"I'll beat you for a tiger."

The moon hung fiery orange, low and heavy in the black sky, beyond the criss-cross of dark tree limbs and shining wires. Erich paid and slid onto the stool with the easy grace he displayed in art class, getting into the corner of the table we shared.

We horsed around on the seats, punching each other in the arm to screw with aim, shouting insults, laughing. We lost the first two games. Then Erich beat me. With a crooked smile, he asked for a white tiger.

He pushed the tiger into my chest. "Take care of him for me. You know what my father would do if he saw me collecting stuffed animals."

"You could hide him."

"And if Col. Brach ever found young Rio, he'd throw him away. We can't take the risk of such a terrible fate."

I held Rio, shivering. Erich's eyes narrowed; then he swung out of his bomber jacket. "Keep it," he said brusquely. He wore a heavy sweater over a nice shirt. "My father bought me a new leather jacket. I've been looking for an excuse to wear it, but I couldn't just lock the old

99

bomber in the closet."

Mute, I tucked Rio in the tan jacket, zipping it up to carry him while my hands warmed in the pockets.

We found a haunted hayride at the far end of the carnival. As we stood in line, Erich said casually, "I heard an eighth-grader over at Greene Meadows killed herself last week. You ever think about it?" Hands in his pockets, scuffing leaves on the blacktop, Erich whistled background music from our favorite show, *Battle of the Planets*. His eyes looked bruised in the carnival light. "No," I said softly.

As we stood in line, a small figure pushed toward us—Lindy, in sleek black jeans and a leather jacket, her fashionably short, feathered hair stirring in the wind like a bird's wing. She smiled at Erich. "Your father told me you'd gone to the carnival. Mind if I join you?"

Erich shrugged, his shoulders lifting the red-and-white scarf. He looked skinny without the jacket. "Did you take the Corvette?"

"Care for a ride?"

"I suppose you brought your sister along."

"Why? She's too old for Hal."

"You've only got a learner's permit, Lindy."

She shrugged. "They won't suspend me. Daddy and Judge Breckinridge golf together."

We walked to the wagons. The dark deepened away from the carnival lights. We sat on bales of hay near the back where we could see the wide countryside in the moonlight. I was suddenly glad I'd zipped the tiger in my jacket, so Lindy wouldn't see me holding it like a child. I sat close to Erich, my hands supporting me as I leaned back on the scratchy bale. Lindy pressed close on his other side, holding his hand.

100

We rolled under the arches of the trees, where strung lanterns showed grisly Halloween scenes—witches at the stake, chain-saw murderers, vampires rising from coffins. I wanted to talk to Erich, say something about the holiday we loved. But Lindy pressed too close; and as we came out of the trees, I saw them locked at the lips.

That surge of jealousy and desire—for a moment, I wanted to kill them both.

And in a twisted way, I got that wish.

After that night, I never saw Erich alive again.

•

Halloween dawned bright and clear. The bus took us past valleys of golden trees. One of the pleasures of autumn was hearing the soft call of an owl that lived in our high old trees. I'd lie in bed staring at the moon, waiting for owls to glide past. I dreamed about befriending one, opening my window to let him fly into my room. I'd feed him in secret, stroke his feathers, and leave the window open so he could circle the night, always returning to me.

This Halloween, Erich and I were supposed to meet after school for a costume party at my church. I thought about it all through home room. But by second period, the world had gone insane.

Alex leaned toward me, his round face intent as Mr. Patrick called roll. "Erich Brach just shot himself. You were his friend, weren't you?"

Hastily whispered details: Erich had called Miss Collins, our guidance counselor, threatening to kill himself, sobbing, almost incoherent. Miss Collins had thought she could save him if she kept him on the line. But then his father showed up, and Erich pulled the trigger.

I sat quietly as the class examined *Romeo and Juliet*, with

101

students assigned to read. I wanted to run screaming from the room. Finally, the bell rang.

I put a hand on Alex's arm. "How do you know? Are you sure?"

"They called Lindy to Guidance. She told Karen before she went to the hospital."

"Then he's still alive?"

"Last I heard."

The story emerged as I wandered through a tunnel of pain. From conflicting accounts, four facts agreed: Erich had a lot of inexplicable bruises and absences; he had called Miss Collins in hysterics, a gun in his hand; the gun had gone off when his father arrived, nicking Erich and sending a bone fragment into his brain; he lay in a coma with Lindy at his side.

My stomach clenched so hard I wasn't faking the sickness that sent me to the nurse. When Mom picked me up, I faced the window while I told her. She hugged me. On the twenty-three minute drive to the hospital, I sat in silence, staring while businesses, churches, hills, and trees rolled by, merging into one heartfelt prayer: *Please, Jesus, let him live. I'll do anything.*

Mom dropped me at the hospital, returning to work. Lindy sat by Erich's bed, holding a pale, square hand and looking into his face devoutly, as if afraid he'd die if she stopped.

Erich lay with the sheets tucked around his chest. One arm hung free; that hand belonged to Lindy. The other disappeared in a maze of tubes and wires. Tubes helped him breathe. The livid splotches of old bruises ran like tattoos up both arms. But his face—

They had shaved his beautiful orange hair. His cheeks looked gaunt, hollowed out, as if he'd been on life support for months. His eyes were a mass of bruises so dark it was hard to tell if they were closed. Around his head, a wide bandage stretched, hiding most of his skull.

I walked toward the bed. My stomach knotted. "Lindy?"

Mascara stains blackened her cheeks. She squeezed his hand. "He's in a coma." Fresh tears coursed down the tracks.

I walked around to touch his other hand, gentle around the tubes.

Lindy urged, "Go ahead. It's okay to hold his hand. We're his friends. It might help him."

The night dragged on. Erich's father didn't come. Mom spoke quietly, words I scarcely heard as she persuaded the nurses to let me stay.

My eyes blurred. I wandered in and out of dreams. The most painful were the ones in which Erich woke and smiled at me. As he began to speak, my eyes would flicker to reveal Erich lying there, pale as death—and me leaning forward, crying over his hand.

Morning brought no magic. My eyes burned. I didn't let go of Erich's hand until they forced me to. Erich's father had finally arrived.

Col. Brach stared at his son for a long moment, then looked the attending doctor straight in the eye. "Turn off the damned machines." He stalked from the room.

The doctors tried to pacify me and Lindy, explaining that Erich was already brain-dead. What did that mean? Erich lay on the bed, white, perfectly still, with dark brown staining the bandage where his flaming hair should be.

Lindy draped him, sobbing, "Why, Erich, why? How could you leave me like this?"

Remorse and guilt ate me. I stood frozen while they

103

pronounced him dead. We were ushered from the room. Nothing made sense. Why hadn't he said goodbye?

I went to school, though I felt so dizzy and tired I didn't think I could last the day. When I opened my locker, things only got worse.

A half-folded note sat precariously atop my books, looking as though it had come unraveled when stuffed through the slot. I stood staring, afraid to touch it. Erich's handwriting.

On Halloween, I'd been too excited to stop by my locker first thing, and too upset later. I pressed myself into the narrow opening, unfolding the letter with trembling hands. Through the blur of tears, odd phrases leapt out at me: "I hate to leave you like this. I love you. Maybe one day we'll have a drink together in hell. Don't cry too much. Wouldn't want to mess up that pretty face."

I read the letter over, trying to make sense. Erich had come to school that morning to leave me this note and drop off his library books. He'd planned to persuade Lindy to drive him home and leave him there—how cruel, to involve her in his death. But as he explained, I understood. It sickened me, but I understood.

Erich's father had found my letter. It was clearly from another boy. He'd beaten Erich within an inch of his life. I remembered a week early on when Erich had missed school, claiming flu, and come back wan and quiet. He'd brushed aside my concern. Erich's letter said his father had been pressuring him to marry Lindy, to lead a "normal" life. Erich had seen the look on my face when he kissed Lindy. He hadn't wanted to hurt me, but he couldn't snub her, for fear of his father. He knew I'd written the letter; he recognized my turn of phrase. He'd been glad, but he didn't dare answer.

104

Then Erich described the ritual, and where he'd found it. He stressed our love of Halloween. "I thought you of all people would appreciate this, Hal—I'll escape on our favorite day." He told me how to find the book after he died. He actually begged me not to desert him, not to share our secret.

He must have had a crisis of faith at the end—called Guidance to tell them about his father, seeking protection that came too late. Maybe Miss Collins misunderstood and had her assistant call Erich's father on the other line. Erich would have pulled the trigger when he heard his father approach.

My pulse thrummed in my throat. A desperate sorrow filled me. I hid the letter in the inner pocket of Erich's bomber, near my heart. I could have saved him if I'd had more courage. I didn't think a worse torture could have been invented.

I lay with my head on the desk. I felt so listless, ready to burst into tears. I would have tried to go home sick again, if it hadn't meant disturbing Mom. But I was spared that decision when Miss Collins sent a clerk for me.

I hung back near the door as I saw Erich's father. His shaven head came close to the dropped ceiling. "Why did my son kill himself? Why would he defile his family name? He was influenced, I'm telling you! Look at this depraved little shit!"

"You must calm down, Mr. Brach," Miss Collins said. "I sympathize with your loss. Erich was a bright, likeable young man. None of us can comprehend why he would choose to die. But Hal is a straight-*A* student with a perfect record."

"Erich got mixed up with some cult! You saw the symbols, Lurlene!"

"I saw some unusual markings, yes. But people who commit suicide are not in their right minds. You know that."

"But I don't accept it!" Mr. Brach advanced. "I have reasons, Lurlene! I won't compromise Erich's honor, but you saw what he did! Right in the middle of a pentagram, like he was calling the devil!"

Suddenly, I couldn't stand it. Rage boiled over. "He was in a lot more pain than we are! We should have helped him! Miss Collins, you don't know what it was like! Erich didn't dare slip up—even get a *C*—for fear of his father! I've seen the bruises. Why do you think he stayed home sick so much?"

She looked haggard, her eyes dark with sleeplessness. "Those are very serious charges, Hal."

His face beet red, Erich's father punched me in the mouth.

And that's how I got to stay home for the next few days.

That first night, the moon rose high over the house, a sliver that slid into my heart with quiet agony, to lodge there like a splinter. So much beauty. And Erich dead.

I said as many prayers as I could think of, concentrating on his face, calling his name softly, begging, pleading that he not be dead. Sometime during that night, the first snow fell like the blankness that froze my heart.

If I could have chosen, I would never have left my room.

When I returned to school, the investigation had already moved beyond Erich's father, a military hero whom none wished to accuse in his hour of grief. I had not told anyone about the note. It had been Erich's secret, and now mine. But it filled me with rage. Now that I knew what had happened, I could see Erich, his feet

106

staked to the dirt in the basement, his blood painting his fair skin crimson where he had slashed the symbols across chest and stomach before falling back spread-eagled within his pentagram of salt and feathers. A revolver in his hand would insure that the change came quickly; but he'd gotten frightened, had second thoughts; and then his father came home too soon. The shot went awry. He died in the hospital, the plan incomplete.

I tried to tamp down my rage against Erich as I looked for his book in the library. Here I'd found novels that both of us loved, Ray Bradbury's *Halloween Tree* and Roger Zelazny's *Madwand*. Erich himself had introduced me to a frightening series of books featuring demons, cursed objects, and ghosts. Most of the books were dusty and nondescript, but they had at least a word on the spine to identify them.

At last I found one that did not. Nothing but a call number engraved in white upon faded black buckram. Nothing on the cover. On the title page, only a pentagram.

I carried it to the counter. The librarian looked it over. No card in the back. Nothing, as she flipped the pages, to indicate ownership.

"Why, this isn't our book at all," she said, holding it out with two fingers, as though she didn't like to touch it. "It must be a discard from some other library. See, this isn't even our classification system," and she pointed to the stenciled number.

I took it from her, involuntarily repulsed as my hand brushed the cover. I clutched the book tightly. It was my last link to Erich. And the foolish, asinine, tragic thing that he did.

•

Each day, I rushed through my homework; each evening, I sat up late while my youngest brother, Ralph, slept in the room we shared. Written so densely, the book confounded my understanding. I felt I was stretching the limits of my mind and still straining to catch the consequences.

The book taught me what Erich had tried. His self-sacrifice on the brink of All Hallow's would not simply cast off his old life; he would gain a new one, in which he might have the power to live as he chose. His letter had been partly farewell, partly a plea to join him.

I learned how to call the spirit of a loved one, and nightly I kept vigil. I lit the white candles I'd filched from last year's Christmas Eve service. I arranged them on the desk near a self-portrait Erich had drawn for art, then given me in his off-handed way. Though I waited till Ralph slept, I could never be certain he wouldn't wake, and I felt I was living on borrowed time. I continued to plead for Erich not to be dead, no longer sure to whom I prayed. Perhaps to Erich himself.

Even if I'd wanted to, I didn't have money for the supplies for Erich's ritual. Instead, I continued my own in the fervor of hope and passion. I took candles from Mom's emergency supply, from the homes of my parents' friends, from the shut-ins we visited, from the church.

I had nightmares of Erich tortured, becoming a demon, his eyes glazed black, lifeless with malice. His father had called him damned; but now he had damned himself. I would wake myself crying, and I could not halt the slow tears over our sins. But I would not stop. I had to give Erich what life I could—infuse him with my hope, my love, my faith.

Time wore on. The investigation into Erich's death

came to nothing. Despite a small memorial in the yearbook, Erich faded to a sad memory as we moved on to tenth grade.

Yet I still lay awake every night, holding Erich close in my mind as I silently called his name. The owl's mournful cry was the last thing in my ears before I slept.

I was sixteen now, quiet and studious, avoiding clubs and sports and friends my age. I had given up art—too painful, now that Erich was gone. I still daydreamed about jaunty Erich with his flyaway scarf, his funny quips. I invented complex stories of our lives together, as I biked around the yard or lay waiting for sleep. I tricked my heart into believing they were real.

Halloween approached, crowned with flaming glory: the day when the dead speak. If it happened, it would be tonight, on the anniversary of his death. I could not allow doubt to enter my mind.

I took my younger brothers to houses decorated with pumpkins and hay bales, scarecrows and witches made of old flannel shirts and overalls stuffed with straw. Human-sized black cats lurked on porches to screech and yowl.

I went to bed happy but anxious. I sat up staring at Erich's portrait, praying until my eyes crossed, wishing myself dizzy. I opened the windows, despite the chill. Ralph had gone to a Halloween sleepover. I lay wrapped in covers, staring as the last of the candles burned down, the shadows flickering to consume the light.

I don't know when I drifted off. It seemed a moment before I woke, but the candles lay dead and dark. The owl's voice sounded close. I lay listening, my heart full.

In the pointless beauty of the early hours, a shadow fell across the moon. Across my face.

I held my breath. The owl perched on the outside ledge,

peering in. Nothing stood between us.

"Come in," I whispered.

With a grace and beauty that took my breath away, the owl flew silently into the room. He fluttered to the desk. There he sat, his ghostly, heart-shaped face glowing.

I stretched out my hand, and the owl inclined his head. I stroked the soft head, the broad, soft back. A lump rose to choke me, but I did not want tears to cloud such beauty.

And then I was stroking the wavy hair of a boy who sat on my desk, legs dangling, all color leached out of him except for his blue eyes.

"Hello, love," Erich said, with half-lowered lids, and such a slow, sweet smile.

"You're back!" I exclaimed, laughing, as my hand continued to stroke his hair, his arm, his chest. He was pale but perfect. "How?"

He laughed and hopped off the desk. "Don't ask questions," he teased. "Don't you think we've waited long enough?"

"Are you a spirit?" I asked. I thought I would burst. Knowledge cut me keenly—his touch was as cold as the wind and he'd come as a ghostly bird that woke by night.

His teeth flashed as he smiled, even whiter than his cheeks. "No, I'm here for good, like it or not."

"I like it," I answered through chattering teeth. He cupped my face in one hand, his eyes glistening in the moon's monochrome. "I've missed you," I said, gripping his shoulders tight.

His lips sought mine. I thought I would go mad. Erich brushed my hair back and nibbled my shoulder. He ran a tooth over it, and I shivered as though he'd traced a cold stylus over my spine.

110

I pulled back so I could see that beloved face, that jaw-length hair—now white. "What are you? My dream come true, I know. My own owl. But, Erich—"

Watching me, his face grew sober, then sad—with a light in his eyes like anger, though not for me. "I'm sorry I hurt you. I couldn't wait. Too much—pressure. My father hated me for failing to be the perfect son. When he found your letter—he burned it. He beat me. He demanded I marry Lindy. Even get her pregnant first, just so I proved I was a man. And think what hell my life would have been at school. All those jocks—all those rich brats—they would have eaten me alive."

"But, Erich—we could have run away together—or maybe Social Services—"

"He would have killed me first."

"But why the ritual, why—"

My voice broke, but he only grinned. "Why become a creature of the night? You ought to know, love. Your pure wishes completed the magic. Only a saint like you could pray a sinner like me from hell to heaven."

"I think I understand why you killed yourself, but—"

He said, "I didn't do it to be young forever. I just wanted to live without fear. I was crippled, you know. I couldn't love you here. Not living in my father's house."

He motioned me into the open window, where I sat with my legs dangling over the stubble of the frozen field. I hopped down, expecting the crunch of the long grass.

My feet never touched the ground.

Erich held me, his arms laced tight around my chest; when I looked back, I glimpsed only wings. We flew past the highway, over hills dusted with snow. Above me, vibrating through my chest, echoed the hollow hoot I knew so well.

As we hovered above the stark, shadowed landscape,

Erich whispered in my ear, soft as the downy feathers against my cheek. He offered me a choice. We might be together forever; we might help right the wrongs suffered by others like us. A fear nagged at me, nasty as a school rumor, that Erich wanted revenge. But I knew the agony of losing him. Tears frosted my cheeks. The stars, so crisp in all that blackness, seemed to sparkle brighter for the thin air. I remembered Dad's finger pointing out stars as he named constellations, Mom singing to us on long road trips as night rushed past the windows, sledding with my brothers after dark upon snow that sparkled in the moonlight. I loved my family, too. I didn't want to leave them.

I didn't want to die.

"I can't decide," I cried, as we flew over the creek, iced into permanent rills.

Erich swung around without a word. We flew back to wooded streets, to stand outside his father's house, a brick mansion in a cul-de-sac of trees. Erich's skin gleamed milk-pale in the moon. As he stood under the streetlamp, the shadows cost me the blue of those eyes, changing them to black pits. His jaw hardened as he told me why we were here.

"Erich, you don't want to do this."

"I have to. As an example."

"You can't kill your own father."

"He killed me!"

"You killed yourself! I would have done anything for you—"

I clung to him, straining to hold him back. He struggled to walk against my weight. Smooth as silk, cold as ice, his arms slid in my grasp till I held only his narrow, bony wrists.

Erich turned to look at me. Rage tightened his face, but

112

tears glistened in the hollows.

"I love you, Erich. I've loved you for a long time."

He laughed, love and hurt forming a bitter edge. "You know, my father read your letter aloud, before he destroyed it. You should have heard him bark and spit, as though your words were a curse. But it was worth it, to know you loved me."

"I'd give my life for you," I said. "But I can't help you murder someone, even him."

He stepped toward the porch. His shadow fell on the door—an owl with upraised wings.

I hugged him quickly, holding him back with everything I had. The painful tightening of his arms told me I wasn't the only one making sacrifices.

"Let's go," I begged, my voice raw.

He took my hand and led me behind the porch to the wood that smelled so deeply of autumn. Under the trees, his face was lost in darkness, but I could still see him in my mind's eye: the living boy with his good humor and sarcastic wit, who still had a shock of blood-red hair and wore a tan bomber jacket and a flyaway checked scarf. Memory conjured his aquiline, patrician nose, his blue eyes, the tender way he smiled, the dramatic flourishes he made with his hands.

This time, his tongue tasted like blood. I couldn't breathe. I didn't want to. I sank down, his hand gently lowering my head to the moss. As I looked up at the moon through the trees, I had one moment of overwhelming panic, the struggle to breathe at any cost. I wanted to live. I wanted to see my family again—Mom, Dad, my little brothers. I wanted to bring Erich back to life, not join him in the night.

Then he covered me with his wings, and I stopped

wanting anything but him.

I shivered on the ground, sticks poking my back, my sides. The dead leaves tickled and cut my hands. That we should pledge ourselves eternally, here in his father's yard—this should be revenge enough. I drank his kiss; blood filled my mouth. Erich had died painfully, and he groaned in anguish while passing on his gift. His rigid, down-turned lips crushed mine. But when he raised his head, out burst a raucous cry of victory.

His smile shone in the milky light of the moon. Erich, my Erich. With two great thrusts of his wings, we hovered above the trees. His wings brushed my cheek and shoulder like the ends of his flyaway scarf while I choked on breath, the remnants of my life. I lost myself as we spiraled up toward the moon on new wings, the two of us twined like a helix.

When breath came again, I laughed so hard in the arms of my love. Around us, night birds called to one another from the treetops. We flew to join them.

# Doughnut Boy
by Sam Slaughter

If he wanted to be a scientist it all would've made more sense. The thrift store graduated flasks were lined up seven-long on four shelves in Devon's room. Sweat dried like splatter art on the insides of each. The top shelf differed in that the cylinders still held liquid. It smelled like the locker room at the Y to Mike, Devon's father.

Mike wanted to keep the door open, to air out the rankness of whatever the hell Devon was doing, but that made the hallway smell. His wife had tried to make it better, but Febreeze did little. Devon wouldn't toss them, either. They'd tried asking him nicely already.

*It's unsanitary, Son,* he'd told Devon.

*I need them,* Devon said, staring at them over the pile of cheat night chicken skins from KFC on his plate, *I need to keep track.*

•

Devon placed the day's flask in the bathtub and wrung his shirt into it. He'd gotten good at capturing around ninety-five percent of his sweat in each flask. He twisted his shorts, then his compression shorts, then his head and wristbands. It was important to get it all. Devon rarely worked out at the Y because he needed to be close to the bathroom at home. Close to his flasks. He needed to measure. It was bad enough that sweat fell off him when he ran or lifted. He couldn't catch it all, even with towels. Devon told himself at the end of the day that he had done more than even he could see, and that worked sometimes. While he planked, he watched droplets of sweat fall and get sucked up by dirt or the carpet. If the earth consumed not just his sweat, but everyone's, did that mean the earth got fatter every day? Was it transferable like that? He hated to think that the earth had to suffer and get fatter because of him.

Devon picked up his notebook while staring at the four droplets he saw glimmering on the bathtub floor. *Plus four*, he said to himself. The electronic scale waited patiently near the toilet.

•

It happened out of nowhere. Devon started working out. It was great. Someday, Mike thought, maybe they'd run together. Not any of the marathons he did—he still had PRs to catch—but some slower practice runs. Or maybe they could shoot some hoops. Hell, he'd play any sport Devon wanted. A sport was a sport. He remembered sitting outside watching Devon pant after a jog-walk around the block. Next it was two blocks, then three, then after a few months Mike didn't know when his son would return. One day, he found Devon in his garage gym, tentatively lifting one of the twenty-pound dumbbells. It was the proudest moment of his life.

They worked out together sometimes, but Devon preferred to do it alone. Mike could respect that. He adored the times when he was in there and the only thing he could think of was maxing out. When they did workout together Devon would scuttle away after, grabbing the towel and locking himself in the bathroom. It didn't leave any time for father-son gym talk. There weren't cougars in yoga pants pretending to get fit, but they could imagine. Instead, his father guessed, he was probably rushing to jerk off, fresh adrenaline firing up every part of him, like Mike when he was a teen. He knew the thrill of a post-workout release.

•

Thirty-five hundred calories in a pound and you needed to consume roughly twelve hundred to maintain a healthy body. That's what the personal trainer at the Y told Devon during the session he'd paid for with money culled from wages earned at The Doughnut Shack. He'd worked there for three years and in that time had consumed countless doughnuts, earning him the nickname Doughnuts at school. Or Doughnut Boy. It was never Devon. Sometimes it was D.B., and Devon held fast to the illusion that they called him that because of his initials.

He'd stopped eating doughnuts on his sixteenth birthday, his last one being a celebratory see-you-in-hell maple-glazed circle of bacon and chocolate. He wasn't going to be Doughnut Boy any longer. He jog-walked for the first time that day. Devon hated how his thighs slapped together, but he kept going, even if it wasn't actually running yet. Day by day, he went a little further, a little faster. He sweat a little more. The trainer told him to track everything.

*It'll help with little victories,* he'd said, so Devon did.

Numbers, though, weren't enough. Anyone could record numbers. Statistics meant nothing without some physical manifestation of what was lost. So he'd dropped some weight, it didn't look like it to Devon. His mirror still showed the same skin shadows, the same flabby man-tits that made him look like an orangutan. It didn't matter what his mother said. She'd say anything. Instead, Devon decided on the flasks. He'd be able to tell how hard he worked then. Undeniable proof.

•

Skinnier and skinnier. Mike was so damn proud of Devon for dropping all that weight. He was even prouder for Devon shrugging it off like it was nothing whenever it was brought up.

*Look,* he'd tell his wife, *look at how much better he looks.*

*Healthier,* his wife would say, throwing a handful of kale into the blender for his morning smoother.

But where had he gotten those beakers?

Flasks, his wife reminded him. They were flasks. Beakers were long and skinny.

*Maybe he should switch to beakers then.*

His wife wasn't amused.

It was the smell that got to Mike and he brought it up often. Whenever he walked upstairs, even if the door was closed, he could smell them. The scent stuck like latex to the inside of his nose. He'd been around plenty of over-ripe men—anyone who'd ever run a race knew just how bad your balls smelled after twenty-six point two—but this was something else. Mike didn't know what to do. Whenever he tried to bring it up, Devon would ignore him. If his mother brought it up, Devon would respond like any other teenage boy—he'd huff and slam his bedroom door. It was his room and he could do what he wanted. There were nights in bed that Mike questioned his wife regarding why they couldn't just get rid of the jars.

*Flasks.*

Flasks. Why couldn't they just get rid of the flasks? They were his parents, damn it, and they paid the bills and fed and clothed him. They did everything loving parents did. What did Devon need them for, anyway? He wasn't fat anymore. The sweat collection was unnecessary. He just needed to look in a damn mirror to see that.

*We'll buy him another mirror if he wants. We'll buy him six more. Hell,* Mike said, *I'll talk him to Ikea myself tomorrow.*

•

The new mirror didn't work. It didn't show anything different. Devon could stare for an hour, and sometimes

121

he did. He turned this way and that, shifting to find where he had lost inches. It all still looked to be there. He could see it. He could still grab a roll of fat the size of a hot dog from on top of his lowest rib. And his gut? He practically had a love-handleful on each side. He pulled at them, wondering if this was how wings developed. If he pulled enough, would his love handles slow his descent if he jumped from the top of a building? When Devon pressed his stomach, he could feel ripples of muscle below, but that wasn't enough.

*It's just skin,* his friend Claire had said at lunch one day. *Everyone has skin.* She pulled on her own bicep and Devon watched an upside-down alabaster bell curve expand and snap back into position.

*See? Skin.*

Devon shook his head. It was fat, not skin. Skin clung tight to the body.

*Look at athletes. Look at television celebrities.* Yeah, they had trainers and were paid to look good, but Devon could look like them, too. He just had to work harder and eat less. It would be easy. Beans were low-calories and they filled you up. Carrots, too. And tea, he could drink lots of tea. He could cut his calories more—maybe down to eight hundred, just for a little while. Until he got where he needed to be. In the meantime, Devon continued filling the flasks, the levels rising as he spent more after-school hours working out.

•

Devon looked amazing. Mike couldn't remember a time his son had looked this good. It reminded him of his own teenage years, when he could pull down whatever tail he desired—all he had to do was smile and flex and they were on their knees or had their feet hitting the ceiling of his pickup.

Those jars, though. Had the smell gotten worse? He asked his wife daily. She ignored him. He made an effort to avoid Devon's room. He'd just get angry and if he was angry, he wouldn't get sex. If he was pissed at his son, his wife was pissed at him. Mike began longer runs and it was there he decided this all was ridiculous. He wasn't going to let it continue, he'd already let it go on long enough. He was the man of the house and what he said went. He got four mirrors that night and set them up while Devon was lifting. He wouldn't be a dick, he'd do it slowly. Transition the boy.

•

None of the mirrors were working. They didn't show what they needed to. Or wait, no. That wasn't it at all, Devon realized. He wasn't working out hard enough. He'd need to drop down to seven hundred calories. He'd forgotten what it was like to be full. He wondered if his skin would turn orange from all the carrots. As long as it was tight, he didn't care what color it was.

He'd come back from a workout and see the sheets he'd thrown over the mirrors stripped off each day. A week in, there were more. They made an octagon of angles he didn't want to see.

The mirrors had been there four days when, post-workout, he saw his father in his room. He thought he'd heard glass breaking as he walked up the stairs but shrugged it off. Devon saw his father wearing rubber gloves and holding a black garage bag in one hand. His back to Devon. Mike turned slowly, flask in hand, locked eyes with his son, and dropped it in the trash bag. Devon stopped in the doorway. He saw all his work in that bag. His father froze, his lips pulled up in a sneer as if they could plug his nostrils.

What didn't his father get? He needed to track his progress. How would he know how hard he'd worked? The mirrors? They did nothing. Scales lied, too. They were always off. He needed the flasks. Needed them.

The two stared at each other as if for the first time. Without the flasks, it dawned on Devon, he'd need to work even harder. He'd *have* to make the mirrors work. Devon looked at his dresser. He'd need a fresh shirt.

Doughnut Boy

# Wet Rot
by Paul A. Hamilton

Winter in the valley wouldn't be worth a mention except the rain leaks underground and plumps up the bodies, making them stink. In a colder climate, where the air could freeze the drops and harden the ground, we might get a reprieve. Might ice over the stench, lock it away for a few months. Instead, we get the wet rot.

I tell you this so you can understand what Ursula Calhoun was dealing with when she done what she did. And, it's important to know there's not much but two seasons in the valley. You got summer with the humid heat, cooking corpses into steamed and bloated bags of gas and shit. Then you got winter and the rot that fills the whole place with the smell of rancid meat and wet dog. You come off the miserable sticky summer and go right into the soggy rank winter a few times. Everyone says it won't get to them, they'll get used to it; but it does and they don't.

For Ursula it was more than the smell, though. I think we all saw that right off. The whole valley has an ass-clenched edge to it, but down where she moved in—little half-village not worth the name "Edberg" they gave it—it's worse. Edberg is just waiting for an excuse to wind the ropes. Like everyone has secret dreams of being the hangman. Like they'd volunteer to wear the noose except it would mean they'd miss the execution.

She never fit in there, and at the same time she belonged in Edberg.

The towns in the valley aren't too spread out. But if you've got a wagon to pull or you don't want to take a chance on the highway, it's half a day's walk from anywhere to anywhere else. I first saw her heading inland from the high dunes off the seaboard, coaxing some crooked old mule with a cart limping behind. Most any-one but her would have been beating that animal sense-less to get it up and moving. Instead, she had one hand on its rump, whispering in its ear like a lover.

Ursula Calhoun was beautiful, but not in the way of young women. She was a woman of labor, but she didn't stoop. You'd find no tutor in her past except sweat and callused feet, but her speech wasn't uneducated. Her age made her a survivor but she lacked the shifty eyes and core mistrust of a cutthroat. Her hair was black; her skin was brown. When she met folks on the highway her eyes looked right into theirs and she said, "Hail, traveler."

Winter was about over when she first came down. There's a week or so between seasons where the smell isn't so bad, where you might be able to convince yourself it's just the briny scent of the ocean following the wind. I wasn't walking, I was out in the fields doing some collec-tion and didn't expect anyone traveling the road to say anything anyhow.

"Hail, collector," Ursula said.

"Hallo," I replied.

"How far to the next town?"

I leaned on my shovel. "Town? Next town's in the middle of the valley. Couple more days from here. Place called Unionville Harbor."

"I see."

"'Course, if you only want a place to stop for the night or day or pick up some work, Edberg is ten minutes in-land and then half an hour north on the creekside trail."

She considered this, then nodded at me with a smile she didn't put much effort into.

"Well, thank you, sir."

"Ayep. Safe travels," I said.

I know it wasn't my fault, but I do sometimes wish I'd said nothing to her that day. Maybe told her instead about Juniper Township about halfway between the creek trail and Unionville. She wouldn't have fit any better with that bunch of criminals. I wonder if having her throat slit for her mule or her head bashed in for the rings on her fingers wouldn't have been the mercy after all.

I remember staring at the gray sky for a long time and then calling after her, "Might want to hurry. Looks like rain soon."

She didn't reply. Could be, she never even heard me.

•

I wasn't there when Ursula Calhoun arrived in Edberg, but the innkeeper, man named Agaton told it to me like this:

"She come in with rolling eyes, like a horse in a thunderstorm. Ordered mead and grapes. We laughed at that. I gave her barley stew and slough ale like everybody else. She asked about the town. Asked about work. There was coin in her pockets, but I bartered for the silk sash on her waist.

"Anyhow, she ate fast and kept asking questions. Finally Jaquaw says he may have need of a scullery maid out at the mill. She agreed and I figured she'd go back to eating or retire for the night. The road's a long and weary walk.

"But she gets a few sloughs in and starts trembling. And still with the shifty stares all around, like she's seeing things in shadows and don't want to have corners of her eyes no more.

"She says, 'Who's in charge round these parts?'

"I said, 'The Council upholds the law; rest of us mind

our neighbors.' I'm suspicious because talking about the Council don't come up for newcomers until a few weeks on, if then.

"She goes, 'Council, huh? Can I talk at them?' and I laughed and said, 'No'm. You wouldn't want to do that.'

"She nodded so I thought she dropped it, but as I was about to walk outside and have a piss I noticed her talking to Hobie Francis. Now Hobie didn't have much reason to be in the inn like that, but she'd hang around sometimes and carry plates to people when I got busy or cleaned tables for a couple pennies tip. Thinking back, she was probably lifting a few pennies out of pockets, too. But Hobie's head was down close to the new woman's, talking low until I came back from making water. I thought I saw a coin pass into Hobie's palm and I didn't like the idea of that. I told Hobie to run on home and stared at the newcomer until she finished her supper and ale.

"She went upstairs after, and next day took Jaq's scullery job, stayed until the Whole Business.

"But when it was all done, I told everybody—everybody who would listen—I knowed something was wrong with that woman. Right from her first meal here.

"'Course no one listens to ol' Agaton."

•

It has become the common shorthand for everything that happened: the Whole Business. You say it to someone from Edberg—or really anyone in the valley—and they'll know what you mean.

I've thought on it a lot. I believe when Ursula Calhoun took the job with Jaquaw Yolder, cooking for his men and cleaning up his old mill, she already had a plan. She had a patience very uncommon to the valley, a calculating mind

I have to admire. Of course if what she said has any truth to it, she heard something from the first moments in Edberg. And what she was hearing didn't sit well with her. I like to imagine she spent that first night up in Agaton's dusty rented room tossing and turning, trying to decide if she should stop and carry out this plan she was half-forming in her head, or if she should push on.

Then again, could be she made up her mind the second she walked past the signpost at the trailhead.

The thing about her job with Jaq Yolder was it came with lodging, so long as the tiny apartment behind the mill's kitchen wasn't too cramped for her. One thing no one ever heard from Ursula was a word of complaint. But with no real home to keep, she had free time in the evenings.

And she had that gift.

People like Agaton claim they saw it coming a mile off, but that's hindsight making clear what folks are embarrassed to say they missed. If you want to be generous, you might say the folks of Edberg didn't believe Ursula was a medium to begin with. Maybe you'd say they didn't believe in mediums or fortune-telling at all. And I am likely to concede people in the valley—all things accounted for—don't have much of a superstitious streak. Might be hard to think it, but I always believed most of these folks have a good head on their shoulders.

But Ursula knew how to sell herself. Started with a few casual palm readings on the mill workers, for laughs, just to infuriate their wives by the sensual way she caressed their thick palms. She'd get this dreamy sense, like a child eating sugarplums on Christmas morning when the stench is drowned for a few hours by gingerbread from the oven and pine from the fresh-cut tree. When a few gossiping womenfolk stormed over to Ursula's back door to confront her, she soothed them all with readings of their own.

That whole summer, bloated and purple as it was, she took the slow path through her plan. She'd rile some group up by attending church with a short dress that showed her legs, or she'd cause some minor uproar with a blasphemous remark about the Council in earshot of a few barflies. Every time these tiny mobs would come banging on the warped door of her little kitchen-quarters, she'd step out with an easy smile and a penitent attitude. Soon enough she'd be reading fortunes or holding hands and speaking to someone's long-dead Ompa for them. Her eyes rolled back in her head and she'd say something like, "He says to remember the fishin' hole, Jamus," even though she was talking to Filo Gren. Filo's—or whoever's—cheeks would get all wet. They'd always say something like, "Never told no one how he used to call me that," or, "How can you know about the fishin' hole?"

Those angry crowds turned into true believers. By the time the sky clouded for winter and the wet rot started in again, replacing the black reek with a gray and green one, she'd won over most of the town.

•

It was a month or so after the rains began when Hobic Francis got called up to the Council. Like I said, I suspect Ursula already suspected some of how Edberg operated, but things happened fast once she saw it for herself. It didn't help that Hobie was the one to start it off. She latched onto Ursula from that first night in Agaton's inn, and used to sit at Ursula's tiny parlor table long after dinner. They'd talk until her mama had finished the chores without her and there wasn't enough candle left to make it back home. So Hobie'd walk through the mud in the dark and people whispered about her.

Hobie was always a greedy little runt. I asked her to come collecting with me one time. She spent the day ignoring the pockets of the outsiders. Instead she picked thistleberries and complained how bad her feet hurt. But when we stopped in Juniper to trade, her pouch was three times as heavy as mine. She'd switched them. Lazy, greedy, but she had the nimblest fingers I ever saw.

It's not succumbing to embarrassment of hindsight to say I knew she'd wind up in trouble, because I told her Ma as much when I dropped her off after our collection trip. Jezzy Francis, whose husband was on the Council and so pretty much raised Hobie by herself, just shrugged. Like the weight of the world made it hard to lift her shoulders a few inches. And that was as far as I could get involved. One more link in the chain of regret I drag around.

·

Same as when Ursula came to Edberg, I was away when Hobie went to the Council. Jaq Yolder was Council-keeper at the time, and he told it to me this way:

"They accused Hobie of snitching a sack of huntcakes from the bakery. She mighta been able to explain it off—or at least avoid the Council—if she'd picked one story and stuck to it.

"That Calhoun was overly curious from the get-go about Hobie's call up. Council was meeting in the basement of the common hall. Remember how they used to meet up under the church, until the smell got so bad people stopped coming to services?

"Anyhow, I was leading Hobie down to the basement and that woman asked to come with us.

"I laughed and said, 'Only an acting magistrate can accompany the accused.' I remembered that I hadn't asked for volunteers. By that time we'd got lax on some of the official procedures, I guess. Maybe if I'd followed the bylaws a bit better...

"Well, I don't recall if Calhoun tried to volunteer or not. I probably didn't give her much space to jump in there before I pushed that little snipe down the basement and shut the door behind me. I seem to recall Calhoun making some racket, but my recollection is that she was always causing some sort of trouble.

"Don't have many regrets bigger than offering that harlot a job.

"Council went the way it always did, though I felt Hobie took the sentence better than most. She went white as moonlight on a pond, but she didn't holler or make a disturbance.

"I came up and made the same announcement I always made after the Council ruled, 'The Council has sentenced Hobie Francis ... to death.'

"And that damn Calhoun woman made fuss enough for two; far bigger even than Jezzy, Hobie's mother. She offered to pay for the huntcakes; she offered to take Hobie in as her ward; she even offered to take Hobie away from the town as a form of guardian-sponsored exile. We all just looked at her like she was mad.

"You know how it was: the Council dispensed justice. That was what they did. You didn't argue, you didn't barter. What good was a Council otherwise?

"We fought about it. 'She stole a few loaves of bread, Jaq!' She said, 'Surely that's not worth dying over?'

"I came back with, 'If you're so against the Council's verdict, why didn't you volunteer as magistrate?'

"She spluttered for a minute and then said, 'How was I supposed to know her life was on the line?'

"'For mercy's sake, Ursula, you know how this works!'"

•

But the thing we all forgot was, she didn't know how it worked. She had a way of making you feel you knew her for a long time, even if she'd been there since the beginning of summer. This was her first Council and none of us realized until it was too late. I try to remember now what everyone attributed her reaction to. Best I can recall is we thought she was just over-fond of poor Hobie. It made sense, she made us feel she was fond of us all. Spend too much time in Edberg and you forget how you have to keep everyone else at a distance, even your own kin. You just never know.

She reminded us what it was like to care for someone without reservation. I don't even mean love or lust, I mean plain old neighbor-like friendliness and compassion. We had steeled ourselves against such a common thing and we were so starved for it, it blinded us a lot to what Ursula said and did. I think we attributed it to the Council. As much as we took them for granted, as far as we deferred to their judgement, they did nothing themselves. We cast the accusations. We carried out the sentences.

We made believe we didn't like the way things were.

Ursula stormed off and missed the hanging.

As I've been made to understand, it was a good one. They used the high tree and Hobie Francis's head came off clean.

136

•

It's impossible for me not to wonder if the Whole Business might have turned out differently had Phicus Imogen not indulged himself with Hobie Francis.

Phicus was the son of Haven Imogen, the town's undertaker. Phicus and Hobie had grown up together, in a manner of speaking. Hobie tormented that boy, first with cruel barbs and kicks to the shins, which Phicus took with a sloppy-grinned stupidity. Once they reached adolescence, Hobie began to tease poor hideous Phicus, whose scoliosis gave him the countenance of a dwarf-locus branch, twisted and blackened. He loved her something fierce, and his father pleaded with him to leave the girl be and focus on learning the trade.

If anyone took Hobie Francis's death as bad or worse than Ursula, it was Phicus.

I never believed Phicus did all of what they say he did to Hobie's body. No one really knows what happened except Phicus, Hobie, and Haven, who found the boy. But desecrating a body—no matter what extent the desecration goes—is not just immoral. To Haven Imogen, it was paramount to ruination. His steadfast respect for the dead is what kept him in business. No one ever dreamed they could do a better job at caring for Edberg's deceased than he. But now his own son had crossed a line and ruined that reputation.

There had to have been a moment where Haven considered covering it up. I don't think he drew a single stupid breath of air in his life. So he knew the moment he caught Phicus with Hobie's body—thick stitching around the neck to make her whole again in death—he knew if he reported it, he'd be done. He had to understand everything he'd built over the years would collapse the instant he brought Phicus to Council.

But Haven was even more righteous than he was wise. He couldn't have lived with himself for hiding such a sin, for harboring such a monster. So he marched his son out into the rain and cast the accusation right then and there.

If there was one factor in Haven's decision he didn't take into account, though, it was Ursula Calhoun.

.

Ursula had spent the four days between Hobie Francis's hanging and Haven Imogen's accusation quiet and sharp-eyed. She stared down anyone who asked her for a reading; she ignored the frequent knocks at her door after hours. "The dead aren't talking," she'd call from her bed, where she sat with her knees up on her chest and her arms hugging herself tight. She may have known from the first day in Agaton's inn what justice looked like in Edberg. But knowing and seeing are sometimes as similar as kissing a hand and being punched in the teeth.

As soon as she got wind of Phicus's Council call, she raced through the deepening puddles to the common hall and arrived while Jaq was working on the second lock.

"I stand as Phicus Imogen's magistrate!"

Jaq shook his head at her. "No, you don't."

"Yes. I do."

Jaq said to me, "Will you talk some sense into her?" He went back to the locks.

I tugged lightly on Ursula's shoulder, edging her away from the crowd. "Miss Calhoun," I said, "it would be most unwise to stand for Phicus today."

"I don't care! I won't let this boy die!"

"Do you even know what he's accused of?" I asked.

"I don't care what he's accused of," she said, hatred wafting off her like the stink of wet rot from under the common hall. "Someone needs to confront the Council."

"Look, you might have had a case with Hobie Francis, but Phicus is accused by his own father of—" I couldn't say the words. "He did something with Hobie. With her body. The Council will sentence death. There's no question. And if you stand for him, the punishment applies to you, not Phicus. Don't you see? Magistrates accept the punishment for their patrons. You'll be sentenced instead," I said, urgent and insistent. But stony hate clouded Ursula Calhoun's face. Hate for me. Hate for Edberg. Hate for herself. I think she felt if she had volunteered to help Hobie, none of this would have happened. I'm sure she believed if she acted earlier, two young lives might have been saved.

Jaq had the door open and Ursula lunged, planting a foot behind Jaq's heels and pushing him hard in the chest so he sprawled on the cold mud. Phicus looked ashamed and alarmed, and I saw him glance at the treeline a few dozen yards away.

"Enough of this madness!" Jaq shouted.

"Yes," Ursula said, her voice low and dangerous, "enough." She turned apologetically toward Phicus and gave him a short nod. Phicus began running, his curled body forcing him into a loping waddle. No one followed. Then, to the yawn of the basement entrance she said in a bold tone, "Council!"

Everyone shared uneasy glances. The Council didn't like to be disturbed.

The sound of rain filled the long pause before the Council appeared: rain on the common hall's tin roof; rain on the soft, saturated ground; the tapping of rain on straw hats; the blip of rain in full, open-topped barrels.

They emerged from the basement, furious. Their shrunken lips sneering and purple, the corpulent bodies slipped loosely like the skin of an over baked potato. Standing water from the basement bloated their feet, and they brought a putrid, moldy miasma with them. Their red, bloodshot eyes glistened and rolled in dry sockets, an unending well of hate behind each. The eyes turned on the congregation.

They stood there in the rain, drops sliding off their sunken cheeks and filling the hollows of their collar-bones. On the annual Eve Of Hallows, we visited the Council, asking what to expect from the harvest to come. Every year the answer was the same raw silence we knew meant prosperity. But here, in the deep part of winter, the quiet was judgment.

Their arms began to raise. A creak of dusty tendons just reached us through the hiss of the drops on the sod. Those of us gathered shuffled, nervously. At first we assumed they would point at Ursula, who had disturbed their deliberations. But they didn't. The fingers fanned out. Each Council member chose one of the assembled. They condemned us. All of us.

"What have you done?" Jaq asked, still ass-deep in mud. "You've angered them," he said to Ursula.

Ursula's tears embarrassed the rain for its lack of conviction. Her eyes closed and clear snot ran from her nose. There seemed to be an understanding on her face, something she recognized as soon as the Council shambled out of their basement tomb. Maybe a piece in a puzzle she'd been working on since she showed up at Agaton's snapped together. The one question mark in her plan. Tears and the rain gave her face a sheen like she had in the summer when the stove was going. She never looked more beautiful to me.

"We're sorry, Council," someone from the growing crowd hollered, "she's new!" Now we remembered. Now all we could think was how she wasn't one of us, that she was an interloper.

The fingers began to sweep with an agonizing slowness across the faces of the townsfolk. All of us, sentenced for her indiscretion. Screams of terror broke out from the back of the crowd. Children began to weep.

"Enough!" Ursula cut through the racket. "They don't mean you. They don't mean me." She licked her lips and reached into her apron, pulling out a box of matches. She held it up, waited for the labored turn of rotting heads to see what she offered.

Their fingers converged on her. Held for a beat. Then the arms drifted to their sides. They had never relented before. Usually, we'd file the condemned out of the Council chambers according to the wisdom of their judgement.

They began to shuffle back down to the basement. Out of the rain. They took the smell with them. Ursula un-hooked a lantern from one of the night-posts, cupped her hand over the match and lit the lamp. The gas sizzled.

Her eulogy, her defense was a whisper: "At last." She threw the lantern down into the basement, and the sound of shattering glass preceded the airy thump of sudden ignition. We stared. What else could we do? The flames reached the subfloor of the common hall and those closest to the building began to feel the heat, humid and sticky in the downpour. Ursula stopped crying, and it seemed the winter in her eyes had ended. Behind her, screams began to echo from the basement. Jaq opened his mouth to shout, to criticize. Then we heard it. We understood.

141

The screams from below weren't screams of agony or pain.

The Council screamed with joy and relief.

·

They ran her out of town, although there weren't a small number who called for her to visit the high tree. She left with her chin up, and I watched her go, hitching her cart to her old mule. She gave me a sad little wave, and patted the mule to get it going.

Few feet down the lane, it stopped and she stood there, urging it with a few impatient shouts. She tugged on the bridle. Defiant, the mule didn't budge. After a minute she reached into the wagon and pulled out a whip, brand new. She hauled back and lit that mule up.

It set right into motion, and Ursula Calhoun never looked back.

# Lavinia
by Tim Jeffreys

ince the day of her arrival at Llandrindro Cottage, the nearby woods troubled Anna. Whenever she was in sight of a window she found her eyes drawn to the first dark clutch of trees which stood perhaps a hundred paces from the cottage's rear face. Always she had the impression that something, or someone, looked back at her from the cover of the trees. Hywel, her husband, laughed when she told him this, as did his parents who owned the cottage.

Still, they often found Ana at a rear window, gazing out. She could not shake the feeling of being watched, although she never saw anything emerge from the woods—except one day early in the morning when a fox leapt into the open giving her such a shock that Hywel said it was a wonder she'd not gone into premature labour. After this, he chastised her if he caught her standing transfixed at a window. He said she gave herself the jitters and it was not good for the baby. His mother, Gaynor, tried to be kind by suggesting that it was simply a primal instinct, like nest building.

Perhaps—she suggested—Anna was merely trying, in unfamiliar surroundings, to identify any potential threats to her unborn child.

"Mother," Hywel said, "don't encourage her. She's letting her imagination run away with her. She knows the baby will be perfectly safe here."

Despite her fascination with the woods, Anna had no desire to venture into them. She would not even go out onto the field of grass behind the house. Then one weekend Hywel brought Samantha to the cottage. Samantha was Hywel's eight-year old daughter from his first marriage. Anna did her best to get along with Samantha, although she couldn't help feeling that the child intruded on her relationship with Hywel. When Hywel showed Samantha affection, or lavished her with attention, Anna felt jealousy flashing through her although she managed not to let it show. She thought that she should be the focus of his attention. She was eight-month's pregnant after all and could hardly do a thing for herself. And when the baby arrived Anna knew she would find Samantha's presence even more awkward.

That Saturday, Hywel locked himself away with his laptop and his parents went shopping in the village, so Samantha spent the day following Anna around the cottage like a puppy waiting to be taken for a walk. Despite her fatigue, Anna did her best with the girl. For a time she involved Samantha in a game of noughts and crosses, letting the girl win game after game. All the while she stole glances at Samantha and thought how although she was clever and had a pleasant enough character (if a little annoying), she was not at all pretty but actually quite plain. She had Hywel's blue eyes and fair skin, but not his thick dark hair and full lips. Rather, she had the gingery-coloured curls of her mother and the same woman's thin, pensive mouth. There was no doubt Samantha would make her father proud one day (she excelled in school, and often delighted in making Anna feel stupid), but it was clear the girl would never be beautiful.

Not like my daughter, Anna thought, cupping her belly with one hand. She'll be so pretty. How could she not be with me as her mother?

Back in the city, after finding out the baby she carried was a girl, Anna would peer into pushchairs at other baby girls. Some of these babies were downright ugly. Some were cute, but none were as pretty as the girl she imagined herself having.

When Samantha showed no sign of boredom, and kept on drawing new grids for the game, Anna said:

"Samantha, why don't you go and play outside? It'll do you good to get some fresh air."

Samantha brightened, eager to please. "Are you coming too?"

"No, dear. I feel too heavy today. We can carry on with this game when you get back."

"OK." Samantha stood and skipped away. Anna heard the kitchen door open and thought: Oh no, I didn't mean out the back! Concerned, she got up and followed after the child. She arrived at the kitchen door in time to see Samantha bounding off across the field towards the woods.

"Don't go too far! Don't get lost!"

The girl called some reply of assent.

Anna returned to the sofa, meaning to close her eyes for a few moments, but when she opened them again she glanced at the clock and realised more than an hour had passed. Slowly, she raised herself and called out: "Samantha?"

There was no reply. The house remained silent.

"Samantha? Sammy?"

No reply. The kitchen door was still standing open, as she'd left it to let in some fresh air. She could see the sun shining in through the gap. Anna stuck her head outside and shouted: "Samantha!"

The girl was not in the field. Anna thought to rouse Hywel and get him to track the girl down but realised he would be angry, both at being disturbed in his work and at the fact that Anna had let Samantha wonder off alone into the woods.

148

*What was I thinking?*

Now her only concern was to find Samantha, and before fully realising what she was doing she stepped outside and strode across the grass towards the woods. Her heart pounded as she approached the first line of trees. Halting in her tracks, she called the girl's name again several times but received no response.

Left with no other choice, Anna stepped inside the shade of the trees. Dappled sunlight lay about the ground like scattered golden coins. As she glanced about herself, a breeze touched the branches overhead and a few leaves drifted silently down from above.

She called again, then gave a start when her shout was answered by the shrill, mocking voice of a crow. Regaining herself, she stepped further into the woods, she yelled Sammy's name The wind moved the trees. The sunlight swayed on the ground. She followed a trodden path until blocked by the hollowed-out stump of a tree, one side black with fungus.

*Oh where is that girl!*

What would Hywel say if he saw her wondering about these woods? She could easily trip and fall. She could tumble down the ravine. She might lie at the bottom for days before anyone found her. Continuing on, she saw to her left a huge tree had fallen into the ravine leaving its massive earthy base standing vertical. Spiderwebs spanned nearby branches. Anna continued along the vague path until she discovered, to the right, a strange circular formation on the ground beyond which the path dipped steeply down and rose again almost at once. The formation appeared man-made and had been constructed from weaved branches.

*Who could have done that?*

Anna shivered. Then remembering why she was here, she called out with a note of desperation in her voice: "Samantha? Samantha?"

"Here!" came the girl's voice, close by, making Anna jump. She appeared from between two trees on the opposite side of the dip from where Anna stood. She smiled at Anna, then at once bounded down the slope and up again to join her.

"Where've you been?" Anna said, sharply. "I told you not to go far."

"I was playing," the girl said. "The good people were showing me how they make the circles." She trotted off along the path ahead of Anna, singing to herself.

Anna followed. "The what people?"

"The good people. That's what they said I should call them. But they said I should call them that in the hope that they would be good." Samantha tittered.

"What're you talking about?" Anna said. "Did you meet someone in these woods?" When the girl didn't answer, she went on: "Did you meet some other children to play with? Is that it?"

"They weren't children exactly. They were…well…"

"What?"

To Anna's relief they left the woods and stepped out into the surprising sunshine. At once she felt calmer. Samantha looked up at her and said in a casual way:

"I suppose they were fairies."

"Fairies?" Anna asked. She suppressed the urge to laugh. Instead she said: "I see. Fairies."

"They told me I was a very pretty girl," Samantha said as they walked back towards the house. "And they said you're very pretty too."

"Me? So they've noticed me have they?"

"Oh yes," Samantha said. "They've been watching you."

Anna smiled at the girl, but felt a twist of unease. Glancing back over her shoulder, a shiver ran down her spine.

The baby's due date neared. Anna spent much of her time sitting at her dressing table, combing her long hair and noting the changes in her face and body. In the early days of her pregnancy she had attained a new glow. Her hair shone, her face was rosy, her eyes bright, and her breasts fuller. At home in the city she was used to male attention, but after she became pregnant she could walk down the street and feel all the men's eyes following her. Now, in these latter stages, she looked puffy, tired and grey. Men in the street wouldn't have looked twice at her. She could not think of herself as beautiful when she felt so heavy.

One morning, watching her husband in the mirror as he moved about the bedroom, she said to him, "I will be pretty again, won't I?"

"I hope so!" he said, with a laugh. "Otherwise, I'll have to trade you in for a younger model."

"Hywel!" she said, turning on him. "I'm being serious. Why must you be cruel to me when I feel so fat and ugly?"

"Why do you think I divorced Jane?" he said. "She'd let herself go, and then you appeared on the scene so young and full of life."

Anna feigned a small cry of horror. She examined her husband's face in the mirror, wondering for a moment if he was serious. His eyes glittered with mischief.

"Oh you," she said. "What a nasty thing to say."

"You should know I'm only fooling around. Now, I have to go to work for a few hours. That office descends into chaos when my back's turned. They don't know who to turn to when I'm not around."

"My clever lawyer," she said. "If the baby has my looks and your brains— well, there'll be nothing it can't do!"

"That's right," he said, leaning over her and kissing the nape of her neck. "But I do hope it's not the other way around."

Anna laughed. "I would like to give her a pretty name. Perhaps we can call her Lavinia."

"Lavinia?" Hywel raised an eyebrow.

"It's a lovely name. Beautiful. It'll suit her."

He laughed and shook his head before heading for the door. "Whatever you want, my darling."

Anna turned to her reflection in the mirror, her face serious. "Hywel," she said. "Do you think we did the right thing moving here to have the baby? It's so isolated. Shouldn't we have stayed in the city?"

He paused in the doorway, looking back at her. "The hospital's less than an hour's drive away. You'll have plenty of time to get there. Besides, with me so busy at work I need someone else on hand to look after you. Who could be better than my parents? Mum has had three babies of her own and dad has delivered hundreds. You couldn't be in a better place, honestly."

"Well, that's another thing that bothers me," Anna said. "Your parents should be enjoying their retirement, not nurse-maiding a pregnant woman who can barely do a thing for herself."

"You're not just a pregnant woman!" Hywel said, exasperated. "You're their daughter in law. And that's their grandchild you're carrying. They couldn't be happier having you here. Honestly."

"Well I miss our house. I wish we hadn't had to rent it,

especially not to those Eastern Europeans. Linda from work said she rented her house to a Polish couple when she went travelling and when she got back there was at least three families living there. She said one couple had a mattress in the airing cupboard! Can you believe that, Hywel? They were living in there! In the airing cupboard!"

"Don't be ridiculous!" Hywel said. "We rented our house to a perfectly nice couple. They were dentists, for Gods sake. Very decent people. So stop worrying."

"I can't help it," she said, turning toward the window. From where she was sitting she could see only the very tops of the woodland trees touching against an expanse of sky. "There's something about this place that makes me uncomfortable. I miss seeing people around. It's too quiet here. And I still feel as if there's something in those woods watching me all the time."

"You're being paranoid."

"Sometimes they steal people's children and replace them with a changeling."

"Now what're you on about?"

"I said sometimes they take a child and put some ugly thing in its place."

"Who do?"

"Fairies."

Hywel snorted. "Fairies now, is it? I thought it was just the foxes you were worried about. Now fairies."

"Samantha's seen fairies. In the woods. She told me."

"Darling, Samantha's only eight."

"They would want a beautiful child like ours. We'll have to be careful."

"Anna," Hywel said in a low but firm voice. "That's enough."

153

The following evening Anna's water broke. She stood at the kitchen window, paused in the act of making a pot of camomile tea. She looked down and saw that a puddle of water had inexplicably appeared at her feet, lit by the kitchen lights. She stood for a moment bewildered until the first contraction hit. She hollered in surprise and pain. Hywel's father appear at her side in his dressing gown with his confident air of a retired physician, and Gaynor called for her son to bring the car around to the front of the house. She felt immense relief. Hywel had been right to bring her here. He could never have coped by himself. Hywel would only panic. And she certainly couldn't have a baby on her own.

They had plenty of time to reach the hospital. It would be a further twenty-one agonising hours until a small, naked, purple, wrinkled and wailing body was pressed into her arms.

"A girl!" someone said.

"Lavinia," Anna said in a tired glazed voice, looking at the form in her arms. "Lavinia."


Before having the baby Anna pictured life with her newborn as a time of bliss. She'd imagined herself tired but happy, sitting in a chair with her beautiful girl cradled in her arms whilst everyone fussed about her. The baby's eyes would be open and gazing up at her and there would be some kind of understanding between them, that they were connected, mother and daughter. The reality was not like that is at all. Lavinia cried and cried and cried. She cried all through the day and she cried all through the night. Anna couldn't get the girl to breastfeed. She ended up so exhausted and distraught that Gaynor often took the child away from her, and Anna was ashamed and angry to see that her daughter became peaceful almost at once in her mother-in-law's arms.

"Give it time," Gaynor would say, looked embarrassed and sympathetic and pleased with herself all at the same time. "It's like anything else. You have to learn."

"But it should come naturally, shouldn't it?" Anna said. "She is my daughter, isn't she?"

When she was left alone with Lavinia, Anna would examine her child, looking to see what the girl had inherited from herself. Lavinia's eyes were still closed so she could not yet see if they had her own light blue colouring. Lavinia's hair was only stubble and impossible to tell what colour it would turn out to be. And Lavina's body was still wrinkled and curled in on itself.

"You are mine, aren't you?" Anna would say to her. "You are beautiful, aren't you?"

Then Lavinia would start screaming again and Gaynor would appear saying: "Give her to me, dear."

One evening the sound of Lavinia crying woke Anna from a long nap. Anna went straight to the nursery and turning on the light she saw that the window was wide open and the autumn wind blew into the room and made the curtains flap like flags. Dead leaves fluttered about the windowsill. Rushing to the cot, she saw Lavinia lying uncovered, her blankets kicked off. She was red-facing and bawling.

"Gaynor!" Anna shouted at once.

Picking up the child, she realised that her babygrow was wet. She had soiled herself with what Hywel called a 'nappy-buster'. Lavinia was prone to 'nappy-buster's and Anna sometimes had to change her clothes four or five

155

times a day.

"Gaynor!"

She jogged the baby in her arms, trying to soothe her. She shouted for her mother-in-law again and heard footsteps on the stairs. Gaynor appeared in the room, exclaiming at the sight of the open window.

"I thought you were taking care of her!" Anna said.

"I left her sleeping. Then the telephone rang."

"The window was wide open!"

Gaynor crossed the room and closed the window, shutting out the wind. "I'm so sorry, dear. I did close it. But the catch doesn't always stick."

"Anything could have gotten in!"

"Now then, everything's alright. Panic over. She's probably just hungry."

"She needs changing."

"Do you want me to do it? You can go back to bed."

"No, I'll do it myself. Thank you."

"Alright." Gaynor, appearing not to notice Anna's anger or her sharp tone, stood at her shoulder making faces at the baby. "Oh, look at that. Her eyes have finally opened."

Anna looked down at Lavinia. With all the fuss she had not noticed that Lavinia had her eyes open. They were grey-coloured and full of fury.

Tears began to spill down Anna's cheeks. Gaynor noticed and said:

"Why, whatever's the matter?"

"Her eyes," Anna said. "I thought they'd be blue like mine."

Everyone told Anna that as Lavinia got older she would become easier to manage, but this proved not to be the case. As the months passed, Lavinia's temper actually seemed

156

to worsen. Night and day, she would wake every hour wanting to be fed. Her eyes remained the colour of an overcast day. A gingery stubble grew on her head. She never smiled no matter how much Anna or Gaynor coo-ed over her. She did not make ga-ga noises like other babies. The only sound she ever made were her insistent cries that turned to racking sobs if she was not attended to immediately. Anna began to wonder how she could have possible given birth to such a child.

During her lowest moment, Anna's mind would return to that night when she'd woken from her nap and found Lavinia alone with the nursery window wide open. The night Lavinia had first opened her eyes. It seemed to her that things had taken a downturn after that night. She remembered that day in the woods with Samantha, when Samantha had said she'd seen fairies and that the fairies had been watching Anna. Was that what the girl had said? That they'd been watching her? And hadn't Anna felt uneasy since the very first day she arrived at Llandrindro Cottage?

One Sunday when Hywel was home, Anna watched him as he stood over Lavinia's cot making faces.

"Who's a darling girl, then?" Hywel said.

Lavina responded by unloading loudly into her nappy.

"Oh." Hywel said. He turned to Anna. "I think she needs changing."

"Alright. I'll do it in a minute," Anna said. Then, as Hywel remained standing over the cot, she said to him. "Who do you think she looks like?"

"Well," Hywel said, tilting his head from side to side. "Well. She looks...well...I don't know. She's got your mouth I suppose. And Mum's nose. And my...well, I don't know."

"She's not ours, is she?" Anna said, as much to her own surprise as her husband's.

Hywel was silent a moment, gazing down at Lavinia. When he spoke his voice had a light, humouring tone, but Anna knew he'd been thinking the same thing. "Of course she's ours. She's our little bundle of…er…joy."

"They swapped her. They got in one night and they swapped her."

Hywel glanced up. "They?"

"The fairies."

"Oh, Anna."

"They've taken our daughter, Hywel. They've given us this…this thing. It's a changeling. That's what it is."

"Anna, I think you need to see a doctor."

"You know it's true, Hywel. That thing looks nothing like either of us."

"Don't talk about her like that. She's not a thing. She's our child."

Anna found herself close to tears. "She's not mine, she's…"

"What?" Hywel said.

"She's…why she's…"

"What, dear? What is she?"

"She's ugly."

Hywel asked the local doctor to visit Anna at home, but Anna said nothing to him of her suspicions. She knew he wouldn't understand. He prescribed pills but she would never take them. She had things to do. She had to focus. She had to get Lavinia back from the fairies.

Winter approached. The trees outside the house had shed all their leaves. Anna and the baby spent their days in the reading room next to the open fire because Gaynor insisted it was the warmest room in the house. The schools having closed, Samantha arrived at the cottage and spent most of her time in the reading room too. She would sit in silence with a book in her lap, but every so often Anna caught the girl watching her. Anna suspected Hywel had asked Samantha to keep an eye on her and the baby.

"Do you remember that day you met the fairies in the woods?" Anna said one day.

Samantha looked thoughtful for a moment, then she said: "Oh, that! I was just playing."

Anna narrowed her gaze. Probably this was what Hywel had told Samantha to say if the fairies were ever mentioned. Undeterred, she went on.

"Do you know much about fairies, Samantha?"

Samantha lit up. She loved showing off her knowledge of things. "There are fairies in one of my books. I've read all about them."

"Really?" Anna said, feigning a casual tone. "And does it say anything about changelings?"

"You mean when they take a human child and replace it with one of their own?"

"Yes."

"Of course. The fairies take pretty babies and replace them with some ugly thing that doesn't grow properly and is always in a bad mood. That's how you can tell. The book says that a changeling can fool most people, but a smart mother just knows when a changeling has invaded her house."

"Really. And does the book say how the mothers can get their real children back?"

Samantha opened her mouth to answer, but then she closed it again and her face became serious. She glanced towards the Moses basket where the baby lay sleeping.

"Does it say anything about that?" Anna pressed her.

"Well…" Samantha said. "It's all just make-believe, isn't it."

"But does the book say anything about how the mother gets her real child back, or doesn't it?"

"There are ways," Samantha said.

"I'll bet you remember them, don't you? You're clever like that."

Samantha forgot herself, wrapped up in her own knowledge. "One way is to throw the changeling into the fire. Then it would jump up the chimney and the real child would be returned."

"Like this fire here?" Anna said.

Samantha looked at the flames in the grate, then back at Anna. She nodded.


Anna waited until everyone else in the house slept, then lifted the baby from its cot and carried it downstairs. She movedquietly. In the reading room the fire burned low, but it was still burning. Its light flickered over the walls. As Anna moved towards the chimney, she glanced down at the small form cradled in her arms. The baby's eyes were wide, but she lay silent. She gazed up at Anna and her expression seemed curious.

"I couldn't wake anyone," Anna whispered to the child. "They wouldn't understand. But they'll thank me once I've got Lavinia back. We'll all be so happy then. My sweet little Lavina. My beautiful girl. I don't blame them, really. I don't blame them for taking her. They'd been watching me, you see, and they knew I'd have a beautiful child. They waited. They bided their time. And then they took her. But now I'm going to get her back."

160

The child in her arms made no response.

Anna paused then, and looked closely at the child. For a minute she thought…wasn't that the same heart-shaped face she herself had? And the eyes. Weren't they Hywel's? Not the colour, but…

The baby started to cry then, and Anna thought: *No, no. It is a thing. Not my child at all. My child was beautiful.*

Gripping the baby in one arm, she took the poker from beside the fireplace and poked at the coals with it. The flames sprang up at once and she felt the heat. The baby went on bawling; its cries turning into those awful howls that so played on her nerves. She lifted it in two hands, thinking: *In a moment I will have my Lavinia back.*

The door behind her burst open, and Hywel and his parents rushed into the room. Samantha followed, hanging back in the door space. There were shouts and before Anna knew what happened, the baby was seized from her and Hywel and his father took hold of her arms.

"What the hell are you doing?"

As she was swung around, Anna saw Samantha in the doorway again and shouted at her.

"Tell them! Tell them the truth! You saw them in the woods! The good people, you called them! You spoke to them! They said they were watching me! Waiting! Waiting to take my baby away! Tell them!"

With a distraught look Samantha turned away.

The doctor returned. He prescribed rest and more pills. Anna took the pills this time. She was confined to a rear bedroom. Gaynor brought her meals on a tray. And Gaynor brought the baby which Anna refused when it was offered to her.

"It's not mine," she would say.

161

Tim Jeffreys

Sometimes she sat by the window, staring out at the woods across the field behind the house. Sometimes, usually at dusk when the light began to fade, she thought she saw dark little figures moving about at the fringe of trees. She would lean forward towards the pane to get a better view, but when she did this the dark little forms vanished. One day in spring, she thought she saw a pale, golden-haired child standing for a moment at the edge of the field before vanishing into the darkness of the wood.

She leaned forward and breathed against the glass.

"Lavinia."

# Unthinkable
by Kathleen H. Nelson

J J had a cocky new spring in his step as he headed for school. It was the first morning back after Christmas break and promised to be the biggest day of his life. The thing that would change everything nestled in his coat pocket. He loved the weight of it against his hip. He loved the shape of it and how powerful it made him feel. He desperately wanted to take it out and show it off, but someone was bound to squeal on him for that and that would be the end of his big day because it was against school rules to pull your piece if you weren't in some kind of danger. JJ's dad didn't like that rule. He said it was bullshit, an infringement on JJ's Constitutional rights, and denounced the school board as a bunch of freedom-hating lib-tards every chance he got. JJ liked that his dad was a patriot, but sometimes, especially after Happy Hour or poker night, his patriotism got a little loud and mean, and JJ was glad when his mother finally told him to chill already.

"Hey, JJ!" Jason shouted from across the street. "I hear Santa was good to you this year."

Jason's dad was best friends with JJ's dad. Jason was two years older than JJ and had been packing a Smith and Wesson since his twelfth birthday. He went with Carla, who kept her mom's pearl-handled revolver strapped to her thigh even when she was wearing her cheerleader uniform. JJ's dad said that was hot. JJ just thought it was cool.

"Best Christmas ever," JJ said. "I'm officially a Toter."

Sweet," Jason said, and then started up Carla's driveway. In parting, he waved and said, "See ya on the firing range."

"You bet!" JJ said.

The firing range was one of JJ's favorite places in the world. He'd started going in middle school along with everyone else in his class because the town had a mandatory Gun Awareness program. Some parents didn't want their kids handling guns at such a young age, but the town said, "Everyone needs to be prepared for the Unthinkable, even children." JJ's dad had complained, too, but his gripe was about the type of armaments that the town provided.

"Simulated pistols? Blanks? What's the goddam point? You might as well have them play laser tag." The town said simulators satisfied budgetary and liability constraints, but added that those students who were of age and so inclined were welcome to BYO. JJ's dad didn't think JJ should have to wait two years to train with the real thing, so he started bringing him and a Beretta nine millimeter out to the woods. The first few times, he had JJ shoot at soda cans. Then they stumbled onto a colony of feral cats and the objective changed —"Because in real life, your target won't be standing still".

JJ was a dog person like his dad, but he didn't hate cats, so he decided to aim for their butts. On his very first try, though, he got one in the head. A spray of brains and blood bloomed in the air like fireworks. The sight made JJ feel sick and sad, but his dad let out a whoop like JJ had done something great, so JJ kept on firing. Since then, he'd learned that those cats were a problem, as bad as or worse than dumpster rats, so basically, he'd been doing everyone in town a favor by shooting them. Knowing that made him feel better, but even so, he didn't mind when those woodland field trips with his dad came to an end.

John F. Kennedy Junior High School was enclosed by a chain-link fence topped with razor-wire. The guard at the back gate was drinking coffee and trying to stay warm. To the incoming girls, he said, "Looking good, senoritas!"

167

To the guys, he said, "You dudes be smart and stay in school. Learn from my example!" No one paid much attention to him, JJ included. He was watching a gang of pre-Toters playing Call of Duty or some other war game over by the basketball court. "BLAM, BLAM!" one of them shouted. "YOU'RE DEAD, YOU STINKING TERRORIST!" JJ smiled to himself, remembering how fun those make-believe shoot-outs had been. Now that he had a real gun, all that kid-stuff was behind him.

At his assigned check-point, JJ fell into line to go through security. "Welcome back, students," an administrative assistant intoned over and over again. "Please take your packs off and pull out your electronics."

JJ shrugged his backpack off and unzipped it. It was brand-new, and made of nylon —-another status symbol. Non-Toters had to carry Kevlar backpacks, which weighed a ton even when they weren't filled with books. JJ had grumbled about that back in the day, but his dad didn't want to hear about it. "Quit whining," he said. "You're building muscle."

One kid after the next passed through the metal detector. When it came time for JJ to do so, he pulled his piece from his pocket and handed it to the monitor with a straight face as if he'd been doing it for years instead of the very first time. Mr. Palin looked JJ up and down as if he didn't recognize him and then broke into a grin. "Well," he said, "look who's exercising his Constitutional rights. And with a Glock safe action pistol no less. You can't go wrong with a firearm like this." Then, as he returned the piece to JJ on the far side of the checkpoint, he added, "Glad to have you on our side, Johnny."

"Thanks, Mr. P," JJ said, beaming now.

He stuffed the gun back in his coat pocket and then

headed toward home room. He got stopped several times along the way by kids who wanted to congratulate him on his new status, so he wound up skating into the classroom an instant before the warning bell rang. By then, Ms. Ruel was calling out seat assignments. The desks with the best sight-lines to the door went to kids with guns. Everybody else landed in the Protected Zone. There was no shame in sitting back there if you were under twelve, but once you came of legal toting age, you were expected to take responsibility for your own safety and weapon up. Only geeks, freaks, and gun-hating libtard spawn willingly stayed in P-Zone longer than they had to. And there weren't a lot of kids like that in public school. JJ knew that. JJ was good with that. Even so, he had always assumed that when it came time for him to take his place in T-Zone, he'd do so alone, like a hero being called to duty. It had never occurred to him that a dozen other kids might get firearms for Christmas! By the time Ms. Ruel finally called his name, there was only one desk left in T-Zone, and it was smack-dab in the middle of the room —as close to P-Zone as you could get without actually being in it. JJ shot the teacher a look that was both shocked and offended. Before he could put the protest into words, though, Mr. Rogers abandoned his post in the background and stared him down.

"Is there a problem, son?" he said.

JJ's dad didn't have a lot of respect for NRAides. He called them lunch ladies with guns and said they were fat-assed, minimum-wage posers who liked to play Big Man on Campus. But Mr. Rogers was the real deal, ex-military down to his crew-cut, camos, and M4 carbine. Although he had never raised a hand or even his voice to anyone as far as JJ knew, everyone at JFK both feared and admired him.

169

"No sir," JJ said, lying because there was nothing else he could do.

"Good," Mr. Rogers said. "Then go sit down."

As JJ made his way to his seat, the kid who had been assigned to the desk one row up and over from him offered a consolatory fist bump. "Welcome to No-Man's-Land," Wally Pittman said.

The call to stand for the Pledge of Allegiance came over the PA, providing JJ with an excuse to ignore the outstretched fist. But instead of reciting the pledge with the rest of the class, JJ glared at the back of Pittman's head and wondered what Mr. Rogers had been thinking when he put that four-eyed dweeb up there and JJ back here. If anybody deserved to be sitting in the very rear guard, it was Wally. The kid was a loser with no friends and no prospects. Just last year, he had pissed himself in the locker room when Jason threw a cockroach at him. A roach, for Pete's sake! JJ could only imagine what the little douche would do if the Unthinkable ever came at him.

"Welcome back, kids," Mr. Rogers said, when everyone was sitting down again. "I hope you all had a good holiday. Judging by the crush of new faces in the T-Zone, I'd have to say that a lot of you did. Congratulations to all who made the shift. I'm proud of you for exercising your right to protect yourself. Question: what's the only thing that will stop a bad guy with a gun?"

Everyone knew the answer to that from Gun Sensitivity Class and shouted in unison. "A good guy with a gun!"

"Correct," Mr. Rogers said. "And we're all good guys here, right?"

"Right!"

"As good guys," the he went on, "it's our responsibility to keep our firearms in good working order. So while Ms.

Ruel is distributing this semester's class schedules, I'm going to see how well the Toters have been doing their homework. You know the drill, people. Weapons out!"

A heavy-metal clatter ensued: guns hitting desktops. A few kids seemed to be sweating the inspection, but not JJ. He cleaned his Glock every night before he slipped it between his mattress and the box spring. No, what had his guts in a twist was the wait. If he had to sit and stare at his gun until Mr. Rogers finally made his way to no-man's land, he'd go bat-shit from

wanting to touch it. So even though texting during class was against the rules, he eased his phone out of his pocket and tapped a message to Jason under the desktop.

"NSPEKZN TYM."

"HERE 2," Jason replied. "LEMME C UR GLK."

JJ checked to make sure Mr. Rogers wasn't looking, then snapped a picture of the gun and sent it to his friend. As he waited for a response, he caught sight of Wally Pittman's piece and sent a picture of that, too, along with a caption. "CHK THZ POS OUT."

"A 22?" Jason sent back. "LOL! THT THNG CDNT PUT AN I OUT @ PB RANGE!"

Exactly, JJ thought, his indignation reviving.

"WHZ?" Jason wanted to know.

"WALLY PZ-PNTZ."

" FIGURZ. THEY STIK HM N NOMANZLND?"

Humiliation burned its way up JJ's neck and into his cheeks. He could not bear to admit that he was the one who'd been stuck. So even though it wasn't so, he typed, "GTG, NRAYD CMN."

There had to be some kind of mistake, JJ thought, as his gaze bounced back and forth between Wally's 22 and the back of Wally's head. Maybe Mr. Rogers had misread the registration form that JJ's dad had sent in. Maybe he thought that JJ was the one who'd gotten a pea-shooter for Christmas. That had to be it. That was the only explanation that made sense. As soon as Rogers realized his mistake, he would bump JJ up to a better desk and piss-pants Wally would be low man on the Toter totem pole. But before the NRAide had a chance to make things right, the PA started broadcasting sharp, buzzer-like sounds. An instant later, the overhead lights went out and metal shutters snapped shut over the windows.

"Defensive positions, people!" Mr. Rogers barked.

Forty-two desks tipped onto their sides, tops facing the door. A drill, JJ thought, as he dropped to one knee behind his. The school always held them at the beginning of the semester to familiarize all the new kids in T-Zone with their new role as protectors. And although JJ would never admit it to Jason or anybody else, he was glad for the practice run. As a pre-Toter, he had played games on his phone after taking cover behind his desktop and beneath his backpack, because really, what else was there to do? But the exercise was much different with a loaded gun in hand —more exciting and intense. Now the clamor seemed more like duty calling than some annoying car alarm going off.

A muffled barrage of gun shots rang out —-simulated fire, a usual part of the drill. Sometimes there were simulated explosions as well. Funny how much more real such noises sounded in T-Zone. And funny how JJ had never heard that subliminal thread of screaming before, either. His cell phone vibrated, signaling an incoming text. At the same time, a dozen Disney ring-tones erupted like a chorus of baby birds. Moments later, kids started squealing all at once.

"Mr. Rogers! This is real! It's really happening!"

JJ wanted Mr. Rogers to ask what they meant by that, but he seemed to already know for he'd shifted out of his casual crouch at the far end of Ms. Ruel's desk and into something more focused even before the ruckus broke out. He made a flat-handed gesture, as if he were patting an invisible dog on the head. A heavy silence fell over the room only to unravel at the next round of gunfire.

"Please, Mr. Rogers," a girl in P-Zone whimpered. "Don't let the Unthinkable get us."

"Don't worry," Mr. Rogers said. "Nothing's getting past us. Right, Toters?"

Everyone in T-Zone came back with, "Right!" but instead of the bold commando sound that JJ remembered from past drills, it was more like a watered-down squeak. Pussies, JJ thought. What was the point in having a gun if you were going to wimp out when the time came to use it? JJ's hands were a little slick and there was a sour taste in his mouth, but that was just excitement. He wasn't afraid, not at all. He'd show Mr. Rogers. He'd show everybody. He was a hero, not a zero.

"All right, people," Mr. Rogers said. "On your marks."

With military briskness, JJ aimed his gun at the door and thumbed his safety to off. He'd have to wait until the three lines in front of him were either down or out of ammo before he got to squeeze off a round, but if and when that time came, he'd be ready to go. Not like Pittman. That kid was trembling so hard, he was almost shivering. He didn't belong in T-Zone. His lib-tard parents had probably bought him that 22 because it was the next best thing to having no gun at all.

"Steady now," Mr. Rogers said. "Keep breathing and stay calm."

173

But Pittman couldn't pull himself together. He was even holding his stupid pea-shooter wrong, straight out and tipped to the left like some gangster instead of cupped in both hands like he had been taught on the range. What a loser! He wasn't going to be any help at all against the Unthinkable. In fact, he'd probably panic and shoot the kids in front of him as soon as the door blew open.

Unless JJ took him out first.

The thought came out of nowhere, a seductive whisper that morphed into a Call of Duty fantasy. JJ shifted ever so slightly and took aim at the back of Wally's head. Potential Target In Range. One shot would do it. One shot, and the class would be safe. He tapped the Glock's trigger guard with his forefinger. Friend or foe? Stay or go?

"I don't wanna die!" someone wailed.

Wally Pittman sobbed. As he did so, a giant snot-bubble ballooned from his nose like an alien airbag. An instant later, a familiar darkness started creeping down the inseam of his jeans. That was it, the last disgusting straw. JJ's finger curled around the trigger. He steeled himself for an explosive bang, the smell of gunpowder, and a spray of brains, thinking, you're dead you stinking libtard terror —

Before JJ could complete the thought, the alarm gave way to the sweet bell-tones of an all-clear. An instant later, the overhead lights came on and the shutters peeled away from the windows, letting in the pale light of a cold winter's day.

"The emergency is over," Mr. Palin announced over the PA. "The danger has passed. Please remain where you are until you're instructed otherwise."

"OK, people," Mr. Rogers said. "Stand down."

174

JJ let out the breath that he had been holding, then thumbed the Glock's safety back into place and stowed it in his pocket. An instant later, his phone vibrated.. The text was from Jason.

"OMG", his friend wrote. "THE NRAYD IN CARLAZ CLAZ SHOT 10 KIDS & THN HIZZELF B4 ANY1 CLD GET A SHOT OFF."

"CARLA OK?" JJ typed back.

"YA. FREEKD THO. ME 2. I MEAN, WHAT MAKES SUM1 DO SUMTHIN LYK THT?"

"WISH I NU, DOOD," JJ replied, glancing at the back of Wally Pittman's head. "THERZ JUZ NO PREDIKTN THE UNTHINKABLE."

# The Destriers
by Forrest Aguirre

Forrest Aguirre

J urgen Frieherr von Röthen wore no wig. The roiling cascade of white that channeled back through a charcoal ribbon and into a ponytail were naturally his, long from years, curled by the strength of noble family blood, and white from the shock and horror of war: Not a war he chose, nor a nobility he desired, but his notwithstanding. His craft was war, his sociality formal and public, but his inclinations, those feelings that made him him despite his title, leaned toward peace and introspection. He was the younger son, destined, as was his want, for the priesthood until his older brother, brash Maximillian, lost his life in an effort to keep the honor of his family name. Jurgen was simultaneously the beneficiary and beast of burden for that protected honor. His elder brother had died dueling, which put his family in high regard. It also re-channeled his destiny from that of a small-town parishioner to that of a cavalry officer in the Saxon army. He traded, in his imagination, the scepter for the saber, the mitre for the tricorn, the pulpit for the horse.

In this last exchange, ironically, he found the opportunity for sanctuary and soul-searching that he desired so much. He had learned, at an early age, that a horse was more than a mere farmyard animal. A horse was to be trusted, respected, and loved. A good mount would return that good faith to its rider.

It was the winter of his twelfth year, 1722, that he learned this for himself, took the lesson not from his father's lips to his ears, but from the cold, hard earth to his beating heart. Not that his father hadn't forewarned him.

"If you should become lost, unsaddle the horse and remove the bit . . ."

178

"But if I . . ."

"Ah, ah! You listen to me, boy. I know it goes against all instinct, but do as I say. Remove the saddle, remove the bit. Let the horse lead you. If you have gained his trust, he will lead you home. If you have not gained his trust by not feeding him enough or by beating him too much, he will gallop away and leave you, and you will have lost a horse you didn't deserve in the first place."

Mere weeks after the conversation, he was charged with taking an important invitation across Spreetal to a renowned doctor. The man had treated Maximillian's wounds, all in vain, but gained the favor of Jurgen's father, who would often invite the doctor to their estate for social gatherings such as the upcoming Christmas celebration. He would ride the stallion, Sturmschneide, the distance. The way was relatively flat, featureless almost, save for the trees that grew up from untilled meadows like clusters of needles in his mother's pincushions. The yellowed grass was lightly dusted with snow from previous flurries, but the sky was clear and the air bitter cold, portending a fair, if freezing journey. On the way back, after delivering the invitation and enjoying a cup of tea, however, a mountain squall swept down from the east, blanketing the sky as gray as Sturmschneide's hide and sifting down a windblown blizzard unlike any in recent memory. Jurgen rode until land and sky became indiscriminate and the way unreadable, like a book wiped clean of ink, terrible in its whiteness.

He obeyed his father's advice and, loosening the saddle and removing the bit, let Sturmschneide lead him through the blizzard. The boy wondered how the horse could be so sure of the way, and he began to re-saddle the animal twice before trusting in his father's wisdom and

179

the horse's sense of direction. After what seemed like days (but was merely cold hours), they arrived at the long white fence of the estate, which was drifted under a wall of snow. Walking along the snow wall, they found the carriage gateway and, from there, walked the path home. As soon as they entered the gate, Jurgen removed all of Sturmschneide's tack, allowing him to trot bareback to the stable and a dry bed of hay.

Sturmschneide sired Wolkenbruch, a beautiful grey-dappled Holstein of lean, athletic build. The two had to be kept from one another, since they were both proud and each longed for dominance over the other. It wouldn't do for the Baron's prize horses to injure each other. As Jurgen grew to manhood, so did Wolkenbruch. Sturmschneide faded and was retired to a nearby farm while Wolkenbruch was trained as a warhorse worthy of a noble rider. Jurgen would sometimes visit the farm down the road when he had leave from the academy, but by the time he was awarded his commission, he could hardly stand to see the old stallion pulling a plow, so tire, so demeaned by age. Sturmschneide would die soon, he know, leaving a kernel of fierce loyalty, intelligence, and fiery will in Wolkenbruch, as Jurgen's father had done for him.

So when news reached him, while out on maneuvers, that his father had passed, he rode Wolkenbruch hard, stampeding across the sky, it seemed, back to the borders of Spreetal, to Röthen, to the estate. There was great solace in that flight, a reassurance that stayed with him even as they galloped past the old farm with no sight of Sturmschneide. Jurgen knew, then, that his father's spirit had saddled up the ghost of old Sturmschneide and taken him on parade, prancing through the gates of heaven, his hooves treading the grey clouds of their moisture, which fell from the sky now, disguising Jurgen's tears.

Jurgen was, by nature, a solitary man. He preferred being alone or surrounded by only a few very close friends. There were times, of course, when duty demanded that he don the coronet and execute the administration of his office. But he found a great distaste for the gossip and conspicuous show of such occasions.

Wolkenbruch, like his sire, also preferred to be alone. Outside of the compulsory procreative instinct, he shunned contact with the other horses of the herd.

But when man and horse were saddle together, connected by the rein and bit, each dropped his walls and melded with the other: man and horse in flesh, a centaur in spirit. Jurgen's shouts and clicks were less commands than urgings, suggestions to Wolkenbruch, who either heeded the intimations, which unlocked a wild expression of speed or bounding, or who pushed back on the master, not out of stubbornness, but out of an instinctive care for the rider's safety. The horse knew his limits and those of the rider, while th rider pushed the steed to excel and find joy in that excellence.

Exhilaration was not, however, the mainstay of the trust between the two. Rather, it was shared serenity that came from their familiarity. After his father's death, Jurgen followed Wolkenbruch's lead and fell, quite naturally, in love with a girl of sufficient standing to honor the family name. Agreements were drawn up and Margretta Ritter became the Baronnes von Röthen. She was happy in her station and Jurgen was content to leave her to her socialites and, in fact, let her take the lead in such matters.

In time, she was with child, which was a dangerous predicament in those days. Jurgen spent as much time by Margretta's side as the midwives would allow, until they asked him to wait outside. Taking a more liberal view of their instructions, the nerve-wracked Baron went out to the stable and saddled his steed.

They stayed on the estate's grounds, never leaving its acreage, near enough to be available in case of an emergency, far enough away that the sound of Wolkenbruch's hooves drowned Margretta's cries of agony. Each stomp was a drumbeat calling the child forth into the world, a chant of war, love, and peace. Jurgen could feel his nervousness disappear, trampled under Wolkenbruch's prancing thunder.

They were, for each other, an oasis of peace even in the fog of war:

*"Hai! Pferd!" Jurgen spurred Wolkenbruch toward the Prussian Grenadiers who wheeled to meet the charge. Freiherr von Röthen stretched his line along their front, exposing the horses sidelong to the muskets only for a moment before curving toward the right flank where the enemy was the thinnest.*

*"Schnell!" he yelled, inviting the horse to a full gallop through the storm of musket-balls that whirred past, cutting through the gunpowder cloud that had blossomed from the Prussians' first volley like flowers from a hedge. A whinny and a scream and von Röthen's Leftenant crumpled behind him. A stray artillery shell burst midway through the Prussian line, weakening their resolve just as Wolkenbruch leapt over their bayonets, parting them like small trees. Another nearby explosion should have sent the steed wheeling back to its own line, but the stallion was resolute, trampling a path through the enemy while his rider sought an enemy worthy to cross sabers, as the rules of war dictated.*

*Confusion reigned around him, but it was as if Wolkenbruch had carried them over the fray seeking a match for his master. Behind the line of Grenadiers the smoke dissipated, showing a thin line of cavalry that had held its charge. Von Röthen looked behind to see his men pouring over the weak flank and rallied them with a wave of the saber, leading the wedge stampeding across the field to the waiting Prussians, all of whom struggled to restrain their eager horses, preparing for the onslaught.*

Now, long after the war, Jurgen was finally able to pursue a life of peace, the life of meditation he had always yearned for. He was too old for the ministry, but studied like an acolyte, spending long hours in his study puzzling over the scriptures and philosophy, trying to reconcile Thomasius, Wolfe, and the gospels. He was orthodox in his morality, but a Pietist when it came to his thoughts on organized religion.

One day, while absorbed in an examination of Thomasius' rancor-filled split with Francke, a servant brought news to Jurgen that his son, Alfred, would be arriving shortly from the academy, where he was, like all men of his age and class, studying the arts of war. Jurgen realized at once that this must be a matter of urgency, since exams were still a month away. He left his study and went to the stable, as was his wont at times like these, and greeted Wolkenbruch with a sugar cube before saddling up to ride the grounds. The day was cold and bright when he met his son at the white fence's gate where Sturmschneide had led him so many years ago.

Jurgen admired his son's horse, "Your mare is beautiful, such a bright red mane. Fiery."

"She's no Wolkenbruch, but she'll do."

"Indeed," he smiled, "I'm glad you're here, but your

183

timing is unusual, to say the least."

"Not my timing."

"Eh?"

"This man's timing," he proffered a sealed envelope to his elder.

"And who might this man be who impinges on my time and tranquility."

"Someone whom I think wishes to impose even more, I'm afraid."

Jurgen did not open the envelope.

"You know this man well?"

"No, but he tells me that you know him well."

"And what is the gentleman's name."

"He's a teacher at the academy. Von Settel."

"Von Settel? That little runt? I had hoped to never hear his jackal-yap again. What a nuisance."

He opened the envelope and read aloud as Alfred looked on, shocked. He had never seen this side of his father before.

"'A simple matter of satisfaction regarding your cowardly abandonment of me at Lobositz'."

Alfred looked at his father with a tinge of fear in his expression.

"A challenge?"

"I'm afraid so."

"I shall stand for you!"

"Only as my second, son. Don't you worry about me, Alfred."

"But father, at your age . . ."

"I am still capable."

"I know you don't want to do this."

"I don't. But I will. I'd rather work through this amicably, but I'm certain he wants blood. Von Settel is a fool."

184

"But he's twenty years your younger."

"And fifty years more foolish. Let me tell you why Von Settel is such a fool, Alfred," he held up the card so that Alfred could see the remainder of the challenge. "Von Settel has challenged me, in his own stupid, theatrical way, to a duel . . . with sabers . . . on horseback."

Alfred wondered if this news was meant to relieve him, which it did not. Still, he forced a smile and "I'm sure you'll be fine. I will be your second."

"Excellent. Now take the response back to Von Settel's messenger. It won't do to postpone beyond tomorrow. Since he has chosen weapons, I choose the location. We will fight here, on my land. That way, if I die, I die on the land I love."

"I will relay the message," Alfred said. "But before I go, what is this all about?"

"It is about Von Settel's inability to control his horse in combat, combined with his egotistical need to blame others for his errors. I suppose it also has something to do with him approaching middle age. He wants bravado, I shall give it to him."

The weather should never delay a proper duel and it did not at this time. Large snowflakes had begun to waft down in softly-blown sheets by the time the duelists, their seconds and a small group of retired officers had gathered. The old warriors were there to oversee the proceedings, to ensure that no foul play took place. They looked on the scene grim, hardened, but with a shifting unease that betrayed the fact that they would rather not be there, but with their children and grandchildren around the fireplace, reaping the peace that comes to the lucky survivors after so many years mired in blood and cannon smoke.

185

The opponents were both dressed sharply in black riding coat and breeches, hands covered in heavy gloves meant to grasp the opponent's blade, should opportunity present itself. There was no need for the clean white shirts of a pistol duel, meant to show more clearly when a hit had been scored, so each wore his coat buttoned up to the neck to keep the cold and snow out of their chest and back, though such comforts would be of little concern to one or the other in a few moments. Alfred, inexperienced in actual combat, wondered if the high-buttoned coat might save his father from a beheading stroke. Jurgen knew it would not.

The horses fidgeted. Wolkenbruch seemed frustrated at the lack of movement inherent in the wait for the signal. Von Settel's horse seemed equally anxious, eager to get on with whatever it was their masters were doing.

One of the old men raised a pistol high in the air, then, checking a watch, fired the starting shot.

Jurgen spurred Wolkenbruch, then let loose the reins, riding with his knees, trusting himself to the horse. He pulled his sword arm back and held his off-hand at the ready, trying to anticipate where Von Settel's sword would strike.

Von Settel rode with his face close to his horse's mane, protecting himself from any arcing cut that Jurgen might make. He tucked his sword close in against his horse, low, aimed at Von Röthen's legs.

As the horse's heads crossed the imaginary barrier between one another, Jurgen swung his sword under-hand, knocking Von Settel's blade up and away from his leg. Von Settel's saber curved up, but with his forward momentum, the blade bit into Wolkenbruch's flank as the horses passed. Worse still, Von Settel's stirrup hit Von

186

Röthen's head-on, kicking the older man's boot completely out of its own stirrup. Jurgen, standing tall over the horse as he was, flipped over Wolkenbruch's left side.

The world spun into a sky full of gray trees and dirt-pocked snow. When Jurgen found his orientation, he was head down with his left foot caught in the stirrup. Wolkenbruch, knowing that his master was in distress, slowed down. Jurgen was careful not to cut himself or the horse with the blade of his sword.

He looked back and, seeing Von Settel wheeling around for another pass, hacked at the stirrup leather, severing it and sending himself to the ground. Wolkenbruch, true to his training, put himself between master and master's opponent as Jurgen extricated himself from the tangled stirrup.

Von Settel, despising honor, charged, cutting over Wolkenbruch to try to get at Von Röthen. Wolkenbruch turned around, blocking Von Settel further and allowing Jurgen access to the good right stirrup. Jurgen mounted swinging his saber, careful not to hit his horse and exacerbate the ugly lacerations that striped his friend's back and flank as a result of Von Settel's determination to hack through horse to get to his man. Von Röthen swore aloud that the whelp would pay dearly for this. Von Settel, filled with rage, did not reply, but struck down angrily, again and again, trying to beat his opponent down before he could fully mount the bloodied horse.

In this, Jurgen saw his advantage.

"Keep hacking, pup!" he yelled, which infuriated the attacker further. Von Settel reared his arm back further, preparing to drop an even heavier blow on the old man.

But Jurgen, smoothly and almost subtly, thrust past Von Settel's upraised arm and drew the blade back across the younger man's chest, slicing through fabric and flesh to grate across bone.

Von Settel screamed and his horse reared. He dropped his sword arm to gain control of the mount. It was enough. With the flick of a wrist, Von Röthen buried the width of his blade into the side of Von Settel's neck, two fingers deep.

The challenger went limp and lolled out of the saddle, landing head first on the ground. His horse, after unintentionally planting a rear hoof into the dying man's chest, bolted. Von Settel's second, giving up all hope on his charge, went off after the fleeing horse.

It was only then, after the rush of battle wore off, that Jurgen realized that he was bleeding from his right calf. He must have accidentally cut himself on his initial defensive upswing. His blood mixed freely with Wolkenbruch's as consciousness fled.

*He was simultaneously thrilled and terrified with no anchor to the earth, like looking down from a mountaintop with no mountain underneath. He held desperately on to the Pegasus' black-braided main as hills and valleys undulated below, farmsteads and villages coming and going in blurs as if he were scanning a map, people and livestock too small to discern, flattened against the landscape. The charcoal horse was a cloud, muscles roiling, black hooves clapping out thunder, tail streaming like a jet ribbon behind him. The Pegasus bucked and brayed and scratched the sky. He tried to calm the steed, but this only seemed to anger it further, so he clung to the mane, eliciting a kick that sent him flying off the creature's winged back, tumbling toward the ground, a valley, a village, a well that seemed to rise up like some giant black serpent and swallow him whole.*

188

*He knelt on the ground, black soil punctuated by tiny chasms from which flame shot forth. The air reeked of sulfur, stinging his nostrils. Sweat poured out of his body in sheets. He looked up and fell back from the fiery eyes staring back at him, a pair of red coals burning in the sockets of an ebony skull. The horse was desiccated, skeletal, a tight blanket of skin over a bone frame. Smoke erupted forth from the Nightmare's nostrils as it spoke in a chorus of wailing women's and screaming girl's voices:*

*"I have suffered enough. My insides burn, my flanks have been flayed, I have been held captive in a pen no larger than my frame, tortured as much by my physicians as by my illnesses. Let me go, let me go . . ."*

Jurgen woke with a start. Alfred, who had been sitting across the room, watching his father suffer from fever, unable to do anything but see to his comfort with a wetted cloth, rose and came to his bedside.

"Fever dreams, father." Then, to a servant, "go fetch him a bowl of soup."

The servant left and Jurgen spoke feebly. "Wolkenbruch. How is my horse?"

Alfred hesitated. "He is alive, but badly hurt."

"Have you sent him off to the yards?"

"No. He is not useless, but he will never serve as a charger again."

"No need. He's done his service and then some. I should like to see him."

"In time. Besides, you wouldn't want him to see you like this, would you?"

"One wounded old warrior seeing another? I think we could provide some empathy for each other."

189

"Fine, but first eat some soup, won't you?"

The servant arrived with a piping bowl of chicken soup.

Later, days later, when Jurgen could properly walk without falling down, Alfred took him out to the stable. Von Röthen used an eagle-headed cane to support himself. "Now, my wound makes me feel my age," he laughed. Alfred laughed, but not because of the joke itself. He was glad his father still kept a sense of humor.

Wolkenbruch was penned in a stall, something that Jurgen had not done to him for some time.

"The horse doctor, Schaedel, said that we should keep Wolkenbruch upright as much as possible so that he won't lose strength in his back and legs," Alfred explained.

"Let him out," Jurgen ordered.

Alfred hesitantly assented. He went to retrieve the bit and harness.

"No!" Jurgen was adamant.

"But how will you lead him?"

"I won't," Jurgen said. "He will lead me."

The old man stood by the old horse and laced his fingers into the steed's black mane. They walked together, Wolkenbruch providing support to Jurgen as they exited the stable and hobbled out to the fields.

"His sire led me as a child, he will lead me as an old man."

The horse walked with its master to the white gate as a slow mist descended from the hills. Alfred followed.

At the gate, the horse stopped.

"He's waiting for me to make the next move," Jurgen explained. "I always know when he's letting me take over."

"He's bareback," Alfred said. "You're not planning to ride him, are you?"

"We've ridden together saddles and bareback, through birth, death, war, peace, love, and hate. I could ride him to hell and back or to heaven, like my father and Sturmschneide. But, no, I don't intend to ride him until he comes calling for me."

He struck the horse on the flanks, "Hai! Pferd!" sending Wolkenbruch through the gate and out into the open wild meadows beyond. The old destrier galloped through the fields, halting, but playing freely, running as fast as his old legs and wounded hocks would allow him. He turned to look one more time at Jurgen and Alfred, the son supporting his father, then bolted off toward the horizon, melting into the grey, raining sky, vanishing into the clouds of mist.

"He'll be back," Alfred said.

"I know," Jurgen replied. "I know."

# Bloom
by Anne Carly Abad

Morning introduces strange things—
a wildflower, newly sprouted
tilled by steady rains
in a sparse accretion of dirt in the gutter

a wildflower, newly sprouted
too stubborn to let pass a chance
to root despite so little soil

hardened by steady rains
a child folds fingers into a hollow bud
to mime the motions of eating rice

in a sparse accretion of dirt in the gutter
the flower will let go, but the child
will curl up to wake another day

www.ingramcontent.com/pod-product-compliance
Lightning Source LLC
Chambersburg PA
CBHW020621180626
46810CB00007B/2876